Georgetown Elementary School
Indian Prairie School District
Aurora, Illinois

TITLE I MATERIALS

Aloha,
Kanani

by Lisa Yee

★ American Girl®

For Nicole and Jordan

*Special thanks to Peter Apo and Maile Meyer for their
insights and knowledge of the Hawaiian culture, and to Sue Kanoho
of the Kaua'i Visitors Bureau for her gracious hospitality.
Mahalo to the Kaua'i Monk Seal Watch Program: to Ronalee Eckberg
and Denise Jones; to Donna Lee and Millie Johnson, who showed
me around the island; plus a special shout-out to Tim Robinson for
his invaluable information about the Hawaiian monk seal
and the island of Kaua'i.*

With gratitude to Puakea Nogelmeier for his guidance on the Hawaiian language, and to
the National Wildlife Federation® for advocating on behalf of endangered species.

Published by American Girl Publishing, Inc.
Copyright © 2011 by American Girl, LLC
Printed in China
11 12 13 14 15 16 17 LEO 10 9 8 7 6 5 4 3 2 1
Illustrations by Sarah Davis

Questions or comments? Call 1-800-845-0005, visit our Web site at americangirl.com,
or write to Customer Service, American Girl, 8400 Fairway Place, Middleton, WI 53562-0497.

This book is a work of fiction. Any similarity to real persons, living or dead, is coincidental
and not intended by American Girl. References to real events, people, or places are used
fictitiously. Other names, characters, places, and incidents are the products of imagination.

Picture credits: p. 114–Susanne Pridoehl; p. 116, top–Daniel Levin.

Cataloging-in-Publication Data available from the Library of Congress.

Contents

Kanani Akina lives in
Hawai'i, on the island of
Kaua'i (kuh-WAH-ee), so
you will see some Hawaiian
words in this book. If you
can't tell what a word means
from reading the story, you
can turn to the Glossary of
Hawaiian Words on page
112. It will tell you what
the word means and how
to pronounce it.

Kanani's name is
pronounced like this:
kuh-NAH-nee ah-KEE-nuh.

As the bamboo ceiling fan chugged overhead, Kanani Akina looked at the calendar hanging beside the cash register and let out a contented sigh. Summer had taken forever to arrive, but now, at last, it was here. That meant every morning, Kanani could help out at her parents' store, Akina's Shave Ice and Sweet Treats. It had been in the family for generations, and, as the sign out front said, it was "sorta famous."

Kanani loved the store. Her great-grandfather had built the old wooden structure by hand, and it was one of the first buildings in the small beach town of Waipuna. The metal roof was rusted and the faded green walls tilted, but the building was sturdy and had even withstood several hurricanes.

Kanani enjoyed greeting customers as they entered the store. "Aloha, welcome to Akina's Shave Ice and Sweet Treats!"

First-timers often looked around the store and marveled. A fiery red dragon kite hung from the ceiling near the beat-up surfboard that had once belonged to Kanani's father. On the walls, paintings and prints from the annual Waipuna Arts and Crafts Festival jostled for space. Rows of assorted candies in oversized jars sat on wooden shelves, and old-fashioned glass counters were crammed with fresh-baked goodies like homemade banana muffins and coconut macaroons. Then there was the mochi—sweet and sticky colorful balls of Japanese rice. Akina's had a reputation for carrying the best local treats.

Now two ladies bustled into the store with large baskets. "Kanani, try this!" Aunty Lea cried as she set her basket on the counter. Nestled inside were clear plastic bags filled with candied pineapple rings dusted with powdered sugar.

Kanani reached for a pineapple ring and nibbled. She nodded.

A wide smile lit up Aunty Lea's sun-weathered face. "See! See," Aunty Lea said, turning to Aunty Aimee. "She likes my treats the best."

"Now wait," Aunty Aimee said, motioning to a bulging shopping bag. "Kanani hasn't tried *mine* yet."

"What is it today?" Kanani asked.

"Mango mochi," Aunty Aimee said proudly. "A new recipe."

Kanani took a bite. It was smooth, dense, and chewy, with a light tropical-fruit flavor. She smiled.

"Aha!" Aunty Aimee pointed to Aunty Lea. "See, mine's the best!"

"No, she said mine is!"

Kanani stepped between them. "Both treats are

excellent," she said calmly. "The pineapple is sweet and tangy, and the mango mochi is so creamy and delicious. I know both will sell well."

"You are quite the diplomat," Kanani's mother noted as she watched the ladies leave the store arm in arm. She turned to her daughter. "So, tomorrow's the big day. Do you remember your cousin Rachel?"

Kanani nodded. Her cousin, Rachel Sutton, was flying all the way from New York City to spend a month with the Akinas. "How long has it been since Rachel and I have seen each other?" she asked.

"Four years," her mother said. "It's been four years since the big family reunion. You were six and Rachel was almost eight years old."

"I remember," Kanani said. "We had a lot of fun together. I wonder if Rachel has changed."

"I'm sure you both have." Mrs. Akina handed her daughter a plastic jug of strawberry syrup. "A lot can happen in four years," Mrs. Akina mused as she reached for the pineapple syrup next.

Kanani was careful as she refilled the glass bottles next to the shave-ice machine. "Like Rachel's parents getting a divorce," she said solemnly.

"And your Aunt Jodi getting married again," her mother added.

Aunt Jodi was Rachel's mother. "How come we didn't go to the wedding?" Kanani asked.

"They had a small ceremony," Mrs. Akina explained. "Just Jodi, her new husband, Paul, and, of course, Rachel." She paused. "Now, Aunt Jodi will be on her honeymoon and then moving into their new apartment while Rachel is staying with us. I'm counting on you to make Rachel feel at home while she's here."

Kanani nodded. "I'll make sure she has a great time!"

The rest of the morning sped by. Mrs. Akina worked the counter and cash register, and Kanani's father was in charge of the shave-ice machine. The back wall listed more than fifty flavors of shave ice. Each name was hand-painted on a piece of driftwood.

"Unlike a snow cone, which is crushed ice, shave ice is like powdery snow," Kanani explained to a young couple on their honeymoon.

The couple took pictures as Mr. Akina lifted a heavy chunk of ice onto the machine. The whirl of the blades sliced through the air as soft ice swirled like a mini blizzard. With plastic-gloved hands, Mr. Akina packed the soft ice into a paper cone and shaped it into a tall dome. Then he handed it back to Kanani for the syrups.

Though the bottles were heavy, Kanani poured them with ease. Using quick up-and-down movements, she transformed the white shave ice into a colorful rainbow of banana, honeydew, and mango syrups. She slipped the cone into a bright yellow holder.

"This is amazing," the woman gushed as she took her first bite.

Kanani beamed. She never tired of watching people enjoy their first Akina's shave ice. "It's *ono-licious*," she told the couple. "'*Ono* means 'really tasty' in Hawaiian."

After a busy morning at the store, Kanani set off down Koa Street, the main road that ran through town and along the ocean. She passed a few small, weather-beaten buildings and then veered onto a dirt road. She kept going until she reached a sky blue cottage tucked behind an overgrown garden. Banana and papaya trees grew in abundance, but what Kanani loved most were the plumeria trees. They were covered with flowers, and the air was thick with their perfume.

"Aloha, *keiki!*" Tutu Lani called out from her rocking chair. "Hello, child!"

Kanani bounded up the creaky porch steps
and greeted the old woman with a kiss on the cheek.
As always, Tutu Lani wore her gray hair in a graceful
bun, held in place by a comb adorned with a mother-
of-pearl sea turtle.

"This is for you," Kanani said, handing over a
bulging paper sack.

"Macadamia nut brittle!" Tutu Lani exclaimed.
"Not so good for my teeth or my waist, but excellent
for my taste buds."

As Tutu Lani savored her first bite of brittle,
Kanani told her about her cousin Rachel. "We're pick-
ing her up at the airport tomorrow afternoon. Could
you please make her a lei—a really beautiful one?"

Kanani knew that Tutu Lani's flower garlands
were the prettiest and sweetest smelling. Everyone in
Waipuna went to Tutu Lani for special occasions.

"Let's make one together," Tutu Lani suggested.
"Come by tomorrow, and I'll show you how."

Kanani lit up at the idea. "Do you have extra-
special flowers we could use?"

"How about tuberose or peppermint-striped
plumeria?" Tutu Lani suggested. "Not only will it
smell sweet, but it will be lovely to look at."

"Sounds perfect!" Kanani said. "I can help you

string it tomorrow before we meet Rachel at the airport. Thank you, Tutu Lani. *Mahalo!*"

Tutu Lani's eyes crinkled into a smile. "Mahalo to you, Kanani," she replied as she dipped into the bag for another piece of macadamia nut brittle.

Kanani felt excited as she left Tutu Lani's and made her way along the the trail toward the beach. It would be such fun playing hostess to her cousin for an entire month! Turning off the trail, Kanani climbed a natural staircase formed by several large stones and boulders. At the top of the boulders, she was rewarded by a beautiful sight—the golden sand and sparkling water of 'Olino Cove. Where the waves broke near the shore, Pika, a boisterous boy from Kanani's class, was boogie-boarding with his friends. Among them Kanani spotted a girl with thick black hair.

"Celina!" she called.

The girl perked up when she saw Kanani and ran toward her. "Did you finish your gift for Rachel?" she asked. "Can I see it?"

Kanani dug into her pocket and then opened her hand. "It's beautiful," Celina exclaimed.

"You're just saying that to be nice," Kanani said. The bracelet hadn't turned out the way she had hoped. "My macramé isn't very good, and the puka shells are bunched up in some spots. This is probably the most lopsided bracelet in the history of the world."

"You know that's not true!" Celina said. "Maybe just in the history of Kaua'i."

Kanani laughed. "Great, so I'm just a disgrace to the island. That's good to know!"

"Really, it doesn't look bad. I'm sure Rachel will love it," Celina told her as she tried it on. "I know I would. My mom always says homemade gifts are the best. What about the picture—did you bring it? I want to see what Rachel looks like."

"Here it is," Kanani said, holding up a seashell frame. In it, a photo showed two little girls holding hands and wearing identical party dresses. The taller girl had straight blond hair, and the shorter girl had long brown curls.

"My grandmother gave us the dresses at our family reunion four years ago," Kanani explained. "She thought it would be neat if we matched."

"She doesn't look anything like you," Celina noted. "Is she your for-real cousin?"

"Yes. Our mothers are sisters," Kanani explained. "But Rachel's father is a haole, so that's why she doesn't look like me." A *haole* meant a white person. Kanani's father had been born and raised in

Waipuna, and Kanani got her sun-kissed complexion from him. Her chestnut brown hair came from her mother's side of the family.

"Your haole cousin is from New York, right?" Celina asked. Kanani nodded. "I've heard that every-thing over there is super fast-paced and hectic—and here we're on island time."

"Ah yes, island time," Kanani echoed as she watched a sea turtle plodding toward the water. "Isn't that why people come to Hawai'i—so they can kick back and relax? I bet Rachel's going to love it in Waipuna."

That night, Kanani opened her dresser drawer, reached under her T-shirts, and pulled out a green book with gold edges—the diary her grandmother had sent her for Christmas. She opened to a blank page and wrote,

> Dear Diary,
> Tomorrow's the big day. Rachel finally arrives! I'm so excited, I don't think I'll be able to sleep. We're going to have the best time ever. The only worry I have is what we should do first!

For once, Kanani awoke before Jinx, her rooster, began to crow. Sunshine spilled through the slats of the bamboo blinds. Kanani quickly got dressed and began to pick up her clothes off the floor.

Mrs. Akina passed her daughter's room carrying an armful of fresh towels. She backed up and did a double take. "You're cleaning without me reminding you?" she gasped, pretending to look stunned. "Are you feeling all right?"

Kanani giggled. Although she loved straightening the shelves and sweeping the floors at the store, the same dedication to tidiness didn't always apply to her bedroom.

"Make way! Make way!" a deep voice cried. Mrs. Akina jumped as a futon mattress made its way down the narrow hall. Behind it was Kanani's father.

"This should do," Mr. Akina said, plopping the mattress on the floor in the corner. Kanani noted that her room suddenly seemed much smaller.

"I'll sleep on the futon," she offered. "Rachel can have my bed. It's more comfortable."

Mrs. Akina smiled. "I'm sure your cousin will appreciate your *ho'okipa*."

"My what?"

"Ho'okipa—your hospitality. Now, let's make

these beds quickly before breakfast," said Mrs. Akina.

After breakfast, Kanani gave Barksee, her dog, a bath. Barksee wasn't too keen on the idea and tried to wriggle away, but Kanani persisted. As she brushed his brown and white fur in the sun to dry, she told him, "You want to look nice for Rachel, don't you?" Then she and Barksee headed up the road to Akina's.

Whenever someone Kanani knew came into the store, she'd tell them about Rachel's visit. "My cousin from New York is arriving today," she told Pika as he studied the candies.

"I know," he said. "You've told me about a million times."

"I have not," Kanani huffed. Pika was so annoying. He constantly talked out of turn in school. Plus his long hair was always over his eyes, so Kanani was never certain if he was looking at her.

"So, what's the big deal about this cuz of yours, anyway?" Pika asked. He pointed to a jar and said, "I'll have my regular."

Using the scooper, Kanani filled a paper bag with gummy frogs. "Well, we hardly ever have guests, and Rachel's never been to Waipuna."

"If you want to show her a good time, make

sure you don't show her your face," Pika said with a mischievous grin.

Kanani handed over the bag. "Is there anything else I can get for you?" she asked sweetly. "Like maybe a muzzle?"

An hour before it was time to go to the airport, Kanani and Barksee headed to Tutu Lani's house.

The old woman lit up when she saw them. "Ah, keiki, there you are," she said, smiling broadly. "Look! I just picked these flowers for Rachel's lei."

Fragrant pink and white flowers filled a woven coconut basket. Kanani set down a bag of macadamia brittle and picked up a blossom. She closed her eyes as she inhaled the sweet scent. *This must be what happiness smells like,* she thought.

She watched carefully as the old woman expertly strung the flowers with a long blunt needle. "Now you," she said, handing the needle to Kanani.

Slowly at first, and then with more confidence, Kanani pushed the needle through the center of each blossom. She smiled as the lei began to take shape. After she added the last flower, Tutu Lani securely tied the ends of the lei together.

"This was made with love, so it is extra special," Tutu Lani told her as she handed it to Kanani.

"Mahalo, Tutu Lani," said Kanani. "Thank you. It's beautiful."

"It's not often a cousin comes to Waipuna all the way from New York. Your visitor is my guest, too." Tutu Lani's eyes twinkled. "Now, what do you have in that bag?"

"Oh! I almost forgot," Kanani said, handing over the macadamia nut brittle. "This is for you."

"And this is for you," Tutu Lani replied.

Kanani bent down as Tutu Lani placed a crown of flowers on her head. It matched Rachel's lei.

The Akinas' battered red pickup rumbled onto the highway. It was about an hour's drive to the airport. Kanani cradled Rachel's lei carefully in her lap so that none of the flowers would get bruised. Suddenly she felt a little nervous. She remembered her cousin only vaguely as a tall, sophisticated older girl who could do all sorts of cool things, like ride a bicycle. What would Rachel be like now?

The Lihue Airport was bustling. As she waited, Kanani played *Oops—Ouch!*, a game she and Celina had made up. The goal was to see how many sunburned tourists you could count. Kanani had gotten up to thirty-four when Rachel's plane finally landed.

As the passengers entered the waiting area, Kanani stood on her toes and scanned the crowd. At last a flight attendant appeared with a somber-looking blond girl by her side. Was it Rachel? Yes!

"Over here!" Kanani cried. "Rachel, here we are! It's me, Kanani!"

The girl gave her a weak smile and then thanked the flight attendant.

Kanani rushed up to her. "Aloha!" she exclaimed as she placed the lei around Rachel's neck. "Welcome to Kaua'i."

"We are so happy to see you," Mrs. Akina said, embracing her niece. "Oh my, you look just like your mother when she was your age."

Kanani studied her cousin. Rachel was half a head taller than she was, with ivory skin and blunt-cut blond hair. Her clothes were stylish, too—a short navy skirt topped with a T-shirt and pink blazer, and short black boots. *Boots? In Hawai'i?* Kanani knew that wouldn't last long.

As Rachel collected her luggage, Kanani noted that Rachel had more suitcases than the entire Akina family combined. And all her luggage matched!

On the ride back to Waipuna, Kanani pointed

out all the sights. "That mountain over there is Waia-leale. It's in the center of Kaua'i and it's the wettest spot on earth. Have you ever been to a lu'au before? We're going to one tomorrow. My best friend, Celina, is coming, too, so you'll get to meet her. Oh, Rachel, we're going to have so much fun! Are you excited to be here?"

Rachel didn't answer immediately, so Kanani kept talking. "Our state fish is the triggerfish. The Hawaiian name for it is *humuhumunukunukuapua'a*, can you believe that? We had to learn it in school: humu-humu-nuku-nuku-apu-a-a. It means 'fish with the nose like a pig!'" As Kanani rattled on, Rachel stared silently out the window.

The truck turned off the main highway and crossed a one-lane wooden bridge toward Waipuna. Suddenly Mrs. Akina stopped for some chickens that had taken over the middle of the road. "It looks like they're having a meeting," she quipped.

The truck idled patiently. "Maybe you should honk your horn," Rachel suggested.

"It's considered bad manners to honk your horn here," Kanani explained to her.

Rachel's eyes widened. "Really? In New York, horns honk day and night, and it's no big deal."

17

Kanani tried to imagine the constant noise. She loved the constant sound of the ocean waves, but car horns? She wasn't sure she could get used to that.

At last the chickens were on their way, and so were Mrs. Akina and the girls.

"Aloha!" Mr. Akina called out from the driveway. "Welcome, Rachel!"

Rachel started to climb out of the truck, then screamed and jumped back in.

Kanani tried not to laugh. "That's just Mochi," she explained as the little black and white goat romped around. "She won't hurt you. Isn't she cute? One of our neighbors gave her to me."

"You have a goat as a pet?" Rachel stammered.

Just then Barksee rushed out of the house to greet their guest. Kanani felt proud of how handsome he looked with his coat shampooed and brushed.

"That's Barksee," she told Rachel, who was still sitting in the safety of the truck. "When we first rescued him from the animal shelter two years ago, he was scrawny and flea-bitten. Now he's nice and healthy."

"I don't suppose you have any more pets," Rachel said, looking around nervously.

"Just Jinx, the rooster," Kanani said. "But he's

always hiding, so if you don't see him, I'm sure you'll hear him in the morning. Come on, let's go inside."

Kanani slipped off her sandals before entering the house. When Rachel saw her aunt and uncle take off their shoes, too, she removed her boots and left them outside the door with the rest of the shoes, but she looked nervous. "What if someone steals them?" she asked. "These are brand-new from Bloomingdale's."

"In Hawai'i everyone takes off their shoes before going inside," Mrs. Akina explained. "Your boots will be fine—there's no need to worry. No one here would ever steal them."

Kanani led Rachel down the hall to her bedroom. "I've cleared out half the closet and some drawers. You get the bed," Kanani told Rachel.

"Are you sure?" Rachel asked, looking at the futon on the floor. Kanani nodded. It made her feel good to offer her bed to her cousin. "Okay, thanks," Rachel said as she unzipped her first suitcase.

Kanani sat cross-legged on the floor and watched Rachel unpack. She had never seen so many trendy outfits before. "We dress pretty casually around here," she said, trying to be helpful. "Shorts, T-shirts, that sort of thing."

Rachel just nodded and continued unpacking.

When she was done, she put the suitcases into each other, like the Russian nesting dolls Kanani had seen on display at the library in Hanalei.

"My mom always wears nice things," Rachel said. "You should have seen her wedding dress. It was beautiful." Kanani perked up. She couldn't wait to hear all about Rachel's life in New York. "And Paul gave her a really big wedding ring," Rachel went on. "He gave this to me, too." Rachel showed Kanani a thin gold necklace with a sparkling stone. "My mom has the exact same necklace, only her diamond is much bigger."

Kanani absentmindedly touched the plumeria charm that hung around her neck. It wasn't real gold, so the finish was dull, but still she loved it because her parents had given it to her when she turned ten. Suddenly, Kanani remembered the puka-shell bracelet. When Rachel wasn't looking, Kanani took it out of her pocket and slipped it into a drawer. A lopsided homemade bracelet surely wouldn't be fancy enough for someone who had a diamond necklace.

Rachel yawned and stretched out on the bed. "Do you mind if I take a nap?" she asked.

Kanani felt disappointed but tried not to show it. "No, of course not," she said and went to join her parents in the backyard. Mochi was eating a paper bag he had retrieved from the recycling bin as Jinx poked around looking for snails to eat.

"Rachel is taking a nap," Kanani reported.

"She's been traveling for more than twelve hours," said Mrs. Akina. The ice in a pitcher of lemonade clinked as she poured Kanani a glass. "She's probably exhausted. Let's let her rest."

"What was that?" Rachel cried.

Kanani sat up. For a moment she thought she had fallen out of bed. Then she remembered she was sleeping on the futon on the floor. It was morning—Rachel's first full day in Waipuna!

"Oh, that's just Jinx, my rooster," Kanani said as she stretched her arms. "He crows every morning. And afternoon. And evening. Come on, let's have breakfast."

Rachel took so long showering and dressing that Kanani and her parents had already finished eating and were cleaning up when Rachel arrived in the kitchen. "How did you sleep?" Mr. Akina asked her.

"I had a hard time falling asleep," she admitted. "It was too quiet."

"Too quiet?" Kanani asked, puzzled.

Rachel nodded. "In New York there's always a lot of noise. They call it 'the city that never sleeps,' but actually, I don't think I can sleep without it."

Kanani stared at her cousin. She had some pretty strange ideas.

"Well, you had a long nap yesterday, and it's five hours' difference between here and New York, so you're probably a little jet-lagged," Mrs. Akina said. "Make sure you eat a good breakfast."

"Would you mind if I used your computer first?" Rachel asked. "I want to see if my mom sent me an e-mail."

"Of course, Rachel," Mrs. Akina said. "You can use the computer any time you want." She turned to Kanani and suggested, "Instead of helping out at the store this morning, why don't you take the day off and show your cousin around Waipuna. Now, come sit down and eat."

When Rachel returned, Kanani couldn't tell if she was happy or sad. "Did you hear from your mom?" she asked.

Her cousin nodded. "They're in Paris. She said they have jet lag." Kanani waited to hear more, but Rachel just nibbled on a piece of bread.

"Rachel," Kanani finally said, "when you're done with breakfast, do you want to change into something more comfortable?"

"Is there something wrong with my clothes?" Rachel asked.

"Oh! Not at all," Kanani quickly apologized. "You look so nice!" Rachel's dress looked like something from a fashion magazine. "It's just that we might go to the beach, and I wouldn't want you to get your good clothes sandy and wet."

"These are my regular clothes," Rachel said.

Kanani pushed her concerns out of her mind. She was here to help her cousin feel at home—not to critique her wardrobe.

After breakfast, the girls headed up the road. The farther they went, the more spread out the houses were. Many of the colorful homes sat on low stilts and had lush green plants and flowers growing in the yard. Kanani pointed halfway up a steep hill. "You can see the waterfall from here. It starts as one stream and then farther down it hits some rocks and splits in two. We call it Wailua Falls, which means 'two waters.'"

"I see it," Rachel said, nodding. "It's pretty. My mom once took me to Niagara Falls. It was incredible. Huge, like a thousand times bigger than this. It's so big that it even generates electrical power."

"There's a pool at the base of the falls, and a big tree with a rope. People can swing on the rope and fly past the falls before jumping into the water."

"People have gone down Niagara Falls in a barrel," Rachel said.

"Wow," said Kanani. She was pretty sure no one had ever gone over Wailua Falls in a barrel. "Come on, there's someone I want you to meet." She turned onto a red dirt road.

Tutu Lani beamed as the girls stepped onto her front porch. "Ah, the lovely Rachel from New York City." Rachel blushed. "Aloha, welcome."

"The flowers for your lei came from Tutu Lani's garden. We made it together," Kanani told Rachel.

"Thank you," Rachel said. "It's beautiful."

"You come over anytime, Rachel," the old woman said. "We'll talk story."

"What's that?" Rachel asked.

"It's just friends sitting around and talking about things," Kanani explained.

"When you've lived as long as I have, you have plenty to talk about!" said Tutu Lani.

"I'm not sure I have much to talk about," Rachel admitted.

Tutu Lani gave her a broad smile, her eyes crinkling. "Everyone has something worth sharing. And while you're here, you'll get new stories to take home with you."

After they bid Tutu Lani good-bye, the girls headed back down Koa Street into Waipuna. Without warning, it began to rain.

"Come on!" Kanani grabbed Rachel's hand, and they ducked into the nearest store, Deb 'n' Darren's Wash 'n' Wear.

Rachel eyed the washing machines and dryers. "Is this a Laundromat or a clothing store?"

"Both!" Kanani answered. "There's Uncle Darren." She waved to a man folding shirts. He returned her smile and waved back. "We'll stay here until the rain lets up."

"What if it lasts all day?"

"It won't," Kanani assured her. "The rain usually doesn't last long. My mom calls it liquid sunshine. The best part is, after the rain comes the rainbow."

As if on cue, the rain let up, and when the girls stepped outside, they were treated to a beautiful rainbow arching across the clear blue sky.

"That's Island Gifts. Tutu Lani sells her leis there," Kanani said, pointing to the small building next to a fruit stand. "Rico's Mini Mart is over there—" she pointed across the street—"but we mostly shop at the farmers' market on Thursdays. Here's the Waipuna Kitchen. They make the best plate lunch. It's owned by my friend Celina's family. You'll meet her tonight. She's coming with us to the lu'au." Kanani led Rachel past the restaurant and opened the door of the community center, a low concrete-block building painted blue. "And here's the museum."

"A museum?" Rachel asked. She looked skeptical but followed Kanani down a hall toward the back of the building to a door labeled *Waipuna Museum*.

As the girls walked in, Aunty Lea looked up from her crocheting. When she wasn't making treats for Akina's, she volunteered at the one-room museum. "Aloha, young ladies!" she called out. "Would you like the quick guided tour, the deluxe guided tour, or the browse-on-your-own tour?"

"Aloha, Aunty. We'll just poke around," Kanani said, laughing. "Look, Rachel, this is Jill Sakamoto's first surfboard—she won the Kaua'i Classic Surfing Competition three times. She grew up in Waipuna."

Rachel eyed the beat-up old surfboard and glanced at the dusty photos and yellowed newspaper articles that lined the walls.

"That's the town's first telephone," said Aunty Lea, pointing to an old-fashioned, wall-mounted wooden telephone. "We didn't get electricity here until the 1930s. We're always a bit behind the times here in Waipuna," she added.

Kanani cringed. What was she thinking, bringing Rachel to the museum? An old telephone, a photo of a surfer from the 1990s . . . how could she have thought these might impress her cousin? Rachel probably thought the town was prehistoric. Kanani looked around the museum, with its dingy paint and bare lightbulb. Aunty Lea was right—Waipuna was behind the times.

There had to be something interesting she could show her cousin. But what? "Hey, Rachel," Kanani called, "here's a photo of my family's store. This was taken a long time ago when it was still Akina General Store, before it turned into a shave ice and sweet shop."

"I hear that the baked goods are excellent there," Aunty Lea volunteered.

"They are," Kanani said, giving her a smile.

As the girls left the museum, Aunty Lea cried, "Come back again soon, and bring more people with you next time!"

"Your aunt sure is enthusiastic," Rachel noted.

"She's not my real aunt, but here we call every-one 'aunty' and 'uncle.' It's like we're all one big fam-ily in Waipuna," Kanani explained. "Everyone knows everything about everyone else."

"Yikes, I'm not sure I'd like that," Rachel said. "By the way, if you like museums, we've got lots in New York. There's the Museum of Modern Art, the Metropolitan Museum of Art, the Natural History Museum . . ."

The more Rachel talked, the more discouraged Kanani felt. It seemed as if no matter what she said, Rachel had something bigger or better in New York.

"Come on, Rachel," Kanani said, trying her best to sound upbeat. "Let's go to my parents' store." Kanani didn't know whether they had shave ice shops in New York, but she felt pretty certain they didn't have a place like Akina's.

As she led her cousin across Koa Street to the shop, Kanani suddenly felt embarrassed. Had the building always looked like this? The paint was peeling, and the worn wooden bench resting in front of the store was seriously lopsided. The hand-painted "Akina's Shave Ice and Sweet Treats—Sorta Famous" sign that Kanani loved so much suddenly looked shabby.

"Rachel!" Mrs. Akina called out as they entered. "Welcome to Akina's Shave Ice and Sweet Treats."

Rachel's eyes widened as she looked around. Kanani's did too. No doubt the ancient cash register would be totally out of place in a New York department store. Instead of a self-serve soft-drink machine, Akina's had a rusty old fridge in the back, crammed full of sodas in glass bottles. To make things worse, there were hand-lettered signs everywhere, with some even written on scraps of cardboard. For the first time in her life, Kanani wished that Akina's was sleek and modern.

Rachel wandered wordlessly through the store, stopping to examine the cookies and cakes. She stared at the colorful mochi and the jars of candies. When she spun the old metal postcard rack, it made an awful squeaking noise.

"It's sort of cramped in here," Kanani apologized as she straightened the postcards. "Some of this stuff has been around for forever, I guess. That's why the place looks like this. Sorry."

"No, no," Rachel whispered. "It's perfect."

"It is?" Kanani said, surprised.

"It's really cool," Rachel told her. "We have candy shops in New York, but they're just pretending to be old-fashioned. This is the real thing."

Kanani wasn't sure if Rachel really meant it or was just trying to make her feel better, but either way, she was grateful, and her spirits rose. "Well, you haven't really experienced Akina's until you've tasted what we have to offer," she said, leading her back to the candy counter.

With Kanani as her tour guide, Rachel sampled many of the sweets. She tried the ginger crisps and chewy banana taffy and seemed especially fond of the pineapple hard candies. "I hope you have room for this!" Mr. Akina said, handing over a huge rainbow shave ice. It was so big that Rachel needed both hands to grasp it.

Kanani held her breath as her cousin took her first bite. Rachel closed her eyes, and when she opened them, a huge smile brightened up her face.

"This is wonderful!" she exclaimed.

The door banged, and Celina and her big brother, Seth, burst into the store.

"The waves are awesome," Seth called to Mr. Akina, and the two high-fived.

Kanani explained to Rachel that when her father was younger he used to surf. "But now that Akina's is open seven days a week, he hardly ever surfs anymore."

"Hi, Rachel," Celina said, waving. "I'm Celina, and this is my brother, Seth."

Seth was tall and lean, and his long brown hair was streaked with blonde. He flashed a smile at Rachel, and Kanani thought she saw her cousin blush.

"Seth works at the beach rental shack," Kanani said.

"I also teach surfing," Seth added. "And paddle-board, and snorkeling, and pretty much any sort of water sports you can think of. Want to learn how to surf?"

"No, thank you," Rachel said politely.

Seth shrugged and turned back to Mr. Akina, describing the waves that were breaking just offshore. Celina joined Kanani and Rachel at the candy counter.

"Guess what?" Celina said. "We heard there's

been a monk seal spotted near Waipuna Beach!"

"Seriously?" Kanani exclaimed. "Oh, I'd love to see it!"

"What are monk seals?" asked Rachel. She took another big bite of shave ice.

"They're tropical seals. The Hawaiian monk seal lives only in Hawai'i, nowhere else," Kanani explained. "They sometimes haul out on the beach, but it's been ages since any have been seen in Waipuna."

"Haul out?" Rachel looked confused.

"That's when they come out of the water and onto the sand," Kanani told her. "Some people from the Monk Seal Foundation came to our school and told us all about them."

"They're an endangered species, so it's sort of a big deal to spot one," Celina added. "If you do, you're supposed to call the coordinator immediately, and they send a volunteer to make sure the seal is safe."

Seth joined the girls. He had a bottle of cherry soda in one hand and a chocolate chip shortbread cookie in the other. "You're the New Yorker, right?" he said to Rachel. "How do you like Waipuna?"

"So far I've only seen the museum, plus a couple of stores. I can't wait to see the rest of the shops. And the movie theaters—I love movies."

When Seth, Celina, and Kanani broke out laughing, Rachel looked flustered. "What?" she asked. "What did I say?"

"I'm sorry," Seth said, almost choking on his cookie. "But as far as stores go, you've probably seen all of them. And a movie theater?" He shook his head. "Waipuna doesn't have one, though you can go into Lihue if you have an overwhelming urge to see a movie on the big screen."

"You can always rent movies at the grocery store," Celina said helpfully. "And sometimes on Saturday nights they show movies at the community center."

"Well, what does everyone do here all day?" Rachel asked.

"They go to the beach!" Kanani and Celina shouted at the same time. Laughing, they linked pinky fingers and then pulled them apart. This was their ritual whenever they said the same thing at the same time.

"Sounds good to me," said Seth. "Let's go!"

Rachel hesitated. "I don't have my swimsuit with me."

"That's okay—we can go home and get it," Kanani assured her. "A lot of times I wear mine underneath my clothes. My parents are convinced that I'm really a mermaid."

"It's all right," Rachel insisted. "We can just go."

"But don't you want to swim?" Kanani pressed.

"No, really," Rachel insisted. "I'll just watch."

At Waipuna Beach, the water was so blue that at a distance, it was almost hard to tell where the ocean ended and the sky began. Using the rubber band she wore on her wrist, Kanani put her hair into a ponytail, then waved to the lifeguard before diving in, with Celina close behind her.

Just being in the ocean made Kanani feel happy. For a while she did the backstroke and gazed at a seabird soaring across the sky. Then with strong, confident strokes, she caught a wave and bodysurfed to the beach. "Come on," she called to Rachel when she reached the shore. "At least get your feet wet."

Rachel tucked her socks into her shoes and walked up to the water's edge. She dipped a toe in. "It's warm!" she said with surprise.

Kanani nodded. "Are you sure you don't want to go home and get your swimsuit?"

Rachel shook her head. "That's okay," she said. "I'll just watch you swim. I'm fine right here."

"You can't just watch—everyone here swims.

Poi

After all, you're in Hawai'i!" Kanani couldn't wait for Rachel to join her in the water. There was no better feeling. "Come on, it'll be fun. The ocean's—"

"Just stop," Rachel said. "Not everyone's into swimming!"

Startled, Kanani was speechless. As the waves lapped around her ankles, she watched Rachel grab her shoes and socks and march to the pier. Kanani's face burned red with shame. Offending her cousin was the last thing she had meant to do.

❀

"Aloha and welcome to the Palikai Lu'au!" The young woman greeted Mr. and Mrs. Akina and the girls by draping flower leis around their necks. "Follow this path to the beach," said the young woman with a smile.

Through the trees, Kanani could see the waves lapping the beach. The sky was a golden orange and purple, and the slender silhouettes of the palm trees framed the sun as it began to dip into the water. Kanani took out her camera and snapped a shot of her cousin gazing at the sunset. But when Kanani looked at the picture, she paused. Instead of looking happy, Rachel looked serious, almost sad.

As they lined up with the other guests, Kanani eyed the buffet. There was kalua pig, which had been cooked for hours in a pit lined with hot stones. She knew the meat would be smoky and tender. She saw sweet potatoes, banana bread, and plenty of fresh fruit and poi.

As the girls filled their plates, Celina explained to Rachel, "That's lau-lau butterfish wrapped in taro leaves. That's Portuguese sweet bread. It's really soft and I could eat tons of it. Over there, that's kulolo; it's a pudding made of taro root and coconut milk. That's chicken long rice—it's a stew with chicken, green onions, and clear noodles, Chinese style."

"Celina's family owns a restaurant," Kanani told Rachel. "So she knows a lot about food. Here's the poi—you have to try it."

Rachel eyed the purplish paste with suspicion. "It looks kind of weird."

"Just try a little," Kanani said, putting some on her plate. "There are different kinds of poi," she said as they sat down. "This is two-finger poi, meaning it's sort of thick, but you still need two fingers to eat it. If the poi is really thick, you need only one. Watch." Kanani put her forefinger and middle finger together and scooped up some poi. "Ummm," she said, licking her fingers. "It's good!"

Rachel looked doubtful.

"Come on, give it a try," Celina encouraged as she ate some. "Be adventurous!"

Rachel picked up her spoon and dipped it into the poi. Cautiously, she tasted it. "Eww, it tastes like paste." Rachel gulped water from her glass. "I can't believe you eat this stuff."

Celina tried to hold back a laugh.

"Well," Kanani said, trying not to sound disappointed, "I guess it's not for everyone."

Mrs. Akina interrupted. "Girls, the show is starting!"

Everyone looked up as the musicians began beating the drums. Young men with bare chests lit torches, and dancers wearing grass skirts swept onto the stage.

"Celina and I took dance lessons," Kanani told her cousin as she bit into a piece of banana bread.

Rachel perked up. "Really? Me too! I've been taking ballet for four years, and one of my favorite things in the whole world is to go to the New York City Ballet. Don't you just love ballet?"

"We didn't take ballet," Celina said, and a flash of disappointment crossed Rachel's face. "It was hula.

I'm not very good at it, but Kanani's a natural!"

Onstage, the hula dancers smiled as they moved to the music. Kanani sat on the edge of her chair and mirrored their elegant hand gestures. After several dances, the master of ceremonies announced, "Now our dancers would like to invite some of our guests to come up here and join us!"

There was a rumble of nervous laughter in the audience as the dancers descended from the stage. "Come join us," one said to Rachel. "I'm not leaving this table without some volunteers!"

Kanani glanced over at her cousin, who shrank back in her seat. "We'll go," Kanani offered quickly, grabbing Celina's hand.

"Whoa, no!" Celina said. "I'm a lousy dancer."

"Come on," Kanani insisted, pulling Celina toward the stage.

"Okay, but you owe me!" Celina whispered.

As the lights dimmed, Kanani, Celina, and the other volunteers disappeared backstage. The thrum of the drums grew louder. Suddenly, spotlights flashed on the volunteers standing at center stage. When a heavy-set man wiggled his hips and tried to dance the hula, the audience roared with laughter. But soon it became clear that one of the volunteers actually did know what she was doing. As the dance became more complicated, Celina stood aside with the others while Kanani kept up with the professional hula dancers, matching her feet and hands to their graceful movements. The smile on her face was as wide as it could be.

That night as they settled into bed, Kanani was still glowing.

Rachel pointed to the red alarm clock on the nightstand. "Hey, I have a clock just like that," she said. "Did you get yours from Grandma?"

Kanani nodded. "A couple years ago for Christmas. But I never have to set the alarm. Jinx always wakes me up." She scratched Barksee behind the ears. "Rachel, if there's anything I can do for you, just let me know."

"Well, if you don't mind . . . " Her cousin hesitated. "I feel funny sleeping in the same room as a dog. What if he jumps on the bed?"

Kanani started to protest, but stopped herself. From the first day she had brought Barksee home, he had slept in her room, and although he wasn't supposed to get on her bed, he often did.

"Come on," Kanani said, leading her dog toward the door. "You can sleep in the family room." Barksee looked confused. "I know," Kanani whispered as she gave him a hug. "But Rachel's our guest, and it's up to us to make her feel at home."

Rachel fell asleep right away, but Kanani tossed and turned. Finally she rose and slowly opened her dresser drawer. She held her breath when it made a squeaking sound, and then carefully reached in and grabbed her diary. The bright light of the moon shone through the blinds. Kanani sat on the futon and began to write.

Dear Diary,

I really messed up today. I thought I was doing something nice by encouraging Rachel to go swimming, but I upset her. I'm still not sure why. I apologized twice, but it's still awkward between us. Rachel didn't talk much to begin with, and now it seems like we have nothing to say to each other. I wasn't expecting things to be like this. How are we going to make it through a whole month together?

The next morning, Rachel stayed home while Kanani helped out at Akina's. When she returned at lunchtime, Kanani was startled to discover her cousin standing on the lounge chair in the backyard yelling, "Shoo! Go away!"

"Is everything all right?" Kanani asked.

Sheepishly, Rachel got down. "Mochi started eating that newspaper, and I was afraid he might bite me."

"Mochi doesn't bite," Kanani assured her. She looked over at her goat, who had worked her way past the sports section and was now enjoying the comics. "But she might try to eat your book. Hey, I'm going to the beach—Seth is helping Celina and me with our surfing. Want to come along and watch?"

Rachel glanced at Mochi and closed her book. "Sure, why not?"

A glimmer of hope shot through Kanani. Maybe things would go better this time.

At the beach, Kanani helped Rachel set up a beach chair to read in. As she, Celina, and Seth headed for the water, Kanani looked back. Rachel was writing in a black notebook. *It must be her journal,* Kanani thought. She wondered what Rachel was writing. Was it about her? Would her cousin have good things to say about her? It was so hard to tell what Rachel was thinking.

"Come on, Kanani," Seth called as they paddled their surfboards out toward the break. "Stop daydreaming and start surfing!"

Celina was up and standing on her board in no time, but before Kanani could get her balance and straighten out her stance, she found herself rolling under the waves like a rag doll. When her head finally popped up from beneath the waves, she gasped for breath. Her surfboard was floating calmly nearby.

"Nice try," Seth called out.

"You'll do better next time," Celina shouted as she sat on her board.

Feeling a little shaky, Kanani swam back to her surfboard. The closer she got, the more she realized that she didn't want to try it again. She loved swimming, and bodysurfing was a blast, but getting tossed around in the surf break was scary. Yet Seth and Celina were waiting for her. Her body felt heavy as she climbed on her board and paddled out again.

"Surfing looks pretty hard," Rachel said as Kanani dried herself off. "I saw you go under a lot."

Was Rachel making fun of her? "I'm not that good at it," Kanani mumbled. "Shall we go get a shave ice? It looks like Celina and Seth are going to be surfing all afternoon."

"That sounds great," Rachel said. "I feel like I'm on fire."

When the girls strolled into Akina's, Mrs. Akina looked stricken. "Rachel, you're as red as a tomato!" she exclaimed. "Kanani, didn't you remind Rachel to wear sunscreen?"

Kanani's stomach turned over. For the first time, she noticed that Rachel's skin looked bright red.

"Rachel, go take a shower right away. Kanani, help her get some aloe vera on her skin," said Mrs. Akina. "And next time, girls, please be more careful."

Rachel's sunburn seemed to get redder as the day wore on, and it hurt Kanani just to look at her. That evening Rachel retreated to the bedroom with a book. Kanani wandered into the garage, where her mother was putting a load of laundry into the washer.

"I'm sorry," Kanani blurted out before her mom could say anything. "I've been a rotten hostess. Rachel's sunburn is all my fault. I was supposed to make sure she had a good time, and instead I've made her miserable."

Mrs. Akina let out a sigh. "Honey, I know you're trying hard. I'm sure that Rachel does, too. As for the sunscreen, you know how important that is."

Kanani nodded miserably. "I feel awful. I thought we'd have fun together, but nothing is turning out the way I thought it would."

"Rachel's probably homesick," said Mrs. Akina. "Remember, this is the first time she's been away from her mother for this long, and she doesn't have any friends here in Waipuna."

Kanani sighed. "I want to be her friend, only it doesn't seem like she wants to be mine."

"Sure she does. Rachel just needs a little help settling in," said Mrs. Akina.

"I don't think she needs any help from me," said Kanani. "She seems happier when she's by herself."

Mrs. Akina gave her daughter a squeeze. "Sometimes those who want help the least need it most. It may seem as if she's pushing you away, but you need to show her the aloha spirit."

Kanani followed her mother back into the house and went into the family room to say good night to Barksee. "I don't know how to help Rachel," she told him. Barksee put his muzzle in her hand and looked up at her with his melting brown eyes.

46

Kanani smiled. "You have the aloha spirit, don't you, Barksee. But what am I supposed to do?" Kanani sighed. She would just have to try harder.

After a few days, the girls slipped into a routine. While Rachel slept in, Kanani would head to Akina's. Though she would never say it out loud, it was a relief to get away from her silent cousin.

The door opened, and two familiar figures entered the store. "Kanani, you must try my new macadamia nut cookies!" Aunty Aimee announced.

Kanani took a bite. The crumbly cookie melted in her mouth. "Ono-licious!" she told a beaming Aunty Aimee.

"Here," said Aunty Lea. "Try this. It's a mini orange cupcake with chocolate coconut frosting."

Kanani ate one. "Mmm, this is ono-licious too!" she told Aunty Lea. "I don't know how both of you do it. Every day you bring in something better than the day before."

Both aunties left the store smiling. As Kanani was arranging their baked goods, a woman and a little boy came by. "Aloha," Kanani said. She handed the boy a free cookie.

"Everything here certainly looks tempting," the woman said as her eyes took in the dizzying array of candies, cookies, and other treats.

"We're on vacation," the boy announced as he stuffed the cookie into his mouth. "We want to live here forever!"

His mother laughed. "Well, that much is true. Everyone here is so kind and friendly, it makes us feel right at home."

Kanani smiled at her customers. If only she could make Rachel feel the same way.

"Do you want some lunch?" Kanani asked her cousin from the doorway. It was noon, but Rachel was still in the bedroom.

Startled, Rachel quickly shut her black notebook and looked up at Kanani. "Yes, I guess so," she said. Barksee lay by her side on the bed. Rachel was still wary around Mochi, but she was growing used to Barksee's gentle ways. Rachel didn't run around and play with him the way Kanani did. Instead, they sat quietly together and kept each other company.

"Let's go to Waipuna Kitchen," Kanani suggested. "They have great lunches, and we'll see Celina."

"Okay," Rachel said with a shrug as she stood up. Her sunburn had faded and started to peel, but at least it no longer hurt her. Still, Kanani felt a twinge of pain every time she thought about Rachel's red skin.

"Come on. We'll bring Barksee with us," said Kanani.

As they walked along Koa Street, Rachel asked, "What does Kanani mean? It's Hawaiian, right?"

Kanani nodded. "It means 'the beautiful one.' Some of my dad's ancestors were native Hawaiians, so my parents gave me a Hawaiian name. I'm a mix of Hawaiian and Japanese on my dad's side—"

"—and German and French on our moms' side," Rachel pointed out.

"Yep, I'm *hapa*," Kanani continued. "That means 'a little of this and a little of that.' My great-grandfather was one of Waipuna's first businessmen. He started the Akina General Store."

"Paul, my new stepfather, is a really good businessman," Rachel told her. "He owns a computer company and has offices all over the United States. That's why we're moving into an apartment building with a doorman and our own housekeeper."

Kanani was quiet. She knew her family wasn't poor, but they weren't rich either. Kanani wondered what Rachel thought about her neighborhood with its dirt roads and old homes wth peeling paint.

"Aloha!" Celina shouted as the cousins entered the diner. "We have a great plate lunch today. You want two of them?"

"What's a plate lunch?" Rachel asked.

"Well, today it's barbecued chicken, and white rice with cabbage and broccoli, and, of course, macaroni salad," Celina explained. "My mom makes the best mac salad and uses homemade mayonnaise. Oh, and we have a ham bone we've been saving for Barksee. I'll bring that out to him."

Kanani glanced outside. Barksee was sitting in the shade next to a bowl of water. His tail wagged every time someone greeted him, which was often.

"My mother and I have been to some really nice restaurants in New York," Rachel said as she read the chalkboard menu. "Have you ever heard of the Four Seasons? I've eaten there. And Paul, my new stepdad, took Mom and me to the Sardi's—that's a restaurant that celebrities go to."

As Rachel recounted all the famous places she had eaten at, Kanani tried not to get annoyed. With its handmade curtains and mural of the beach painted on the wall, Waipuna Kitchen was warm and homey.

But the plates didn't match, the silverware consisted of disposable wooden chopsticks and plastic forks and spoons, and each table had a paper napkin dispenser—something Kanani guessed they probably didn't have at Sardi's or the Four Seasons.

"I like noodles, but not with mayonnaise," Rachel was saying. "What else do you have?"

"The saimin's on special today," Celina replied as she cleared one of the tables.

"That's Japanese noodle soup," Kanani explained, "with all sorts of good stuff thrown in."

"I'm not sure," Rachel said, looking uncertain.

"It's got noodles—try it," Celina coaxed. "Don't you love trying new things?"

"Not really," Rachel said truthfully.

"I tell you what," Celina said. "I'll bring you a bowl of saimin. If you don't like it, I'll get you something else. Okay?"

"Okay, I guess," Rachel replied.

When the soup came, Rachel stared at her bowl. She waited until Celina went to get the drinks and then leaned across the table. "I think the cook messed up," she whispered. "There's an egg in my soup."

Kanani laughed. "That's supposed to be there. The reddish meat is called char siu—that's Chinese barbecued pork—and this is kamaboko," she said, holding up a slice of something smooth and white, rimmed with pink. "It's made of fish."

Rachel made a face.

"It's really good," Kanani said. "I guarantee you'll like it much better than poi."

Celina set down big glasses of iced tea and pulled up a chair. "Well?" she asked. "What do you think of our saimin?"

Rachel was already busy slurping noodles, but she managed to nod and give Celina a thumbs-up.

Kanani felt relieved. Now she had found two things Rachel liked—shave ice and saimin!

That afternoon, while she and Celina were paddling out on their surfboards, Kanani said, "I'm sorry for the way Rachel acted at lunch today."

Celina turned to her. "Why? What did she do?"

"You know, how she kept talking about all the fancy restaurants she's been to," Kanani reminded her.

Celina sat up on her surfboard. "Well, I did notice that she loves to talk about New York. But that's okay. Waipuna Kitchen is never going to be a celebrity hot spot, but I don't mind. I like it the way it is."

Before Kanani could say anything else, Celina suddenly pointed and yelled, "Look at that!"

Panic surged through Kanani as she saw the big set of waves building in the distance.

"Wooooooooo!" Celina shouted. "This is going to be fun!" She rose gracefully up on her board.

Kanani struggled to stand, but before she could put her arms out for balance, the first wave rolled under her and tossed her off her board.

As she surfaced, Pika and some of the other boys paddled past her, laughing. "Hey, surfer girl!" Pika yelled. "Wipeout!"

Kanani cringed and turned back to watch Celina and Seth as they paddled toward the big waves. She turned and headed back to shore.

Rachel was sitting in the shade of the lifeguard station. "I don't know how anyone can stand up on a surfboard," she remarked.

"It is hard," Kanani conceded. "But Celina's so good at it, she makes it look easy."

"Kind of like you and swimming, I guess," Rachel said.

"What do you mean?" Kanani asked.

"Well, you swim like a fish. I'm nervous just going in the deep end of a pool, but at least I can always grab onto the side. In the ocean, there's nothing to hold on to. You're so brave, Kanani. It's like you're not afraid of anything. Surfing would terrify me. You must love it out there since you surf all the time."

Is that what Rachel thinks? Kanani wondered. *That I'm brave and love surfing?* Her face flushed.

That night, Kanani wrote,

Dear Diary,

It was fun taking Rachel to Celina's restaurant today and introducing her to saimin. What wasn't fun today was surfing, but I'm going to try to stick with it because of Celina. After all, she took hula with me when she wasn't too excited about it, so I guess fair is fair.

Rachel thinks I love surfing, but I'm not even sure if I like it. She has completely misjudged me.

Barksee waited patiently by the front door with his leash in his mouth. "I'm coming, I'm coming," Kanani assured him. They both looked forward to their afternoon walk. For Kanani it was a chance to clear her mind and think. For Barksee it was a chance to bark at the birds and sniff at the plants, and to sit and extend his paw whenever he saw someone he knew. Kanani recalled that when she had first rescued him, he was scared of everyone and everything. Now Barksee was as outgoing as the other members of the Akina family.

As they neared the entrance of 'Olino Cove, Kanani attached Barksee's leash to his collar. Soon they were jogging along the shore. Sometimes the water looked emerald green, sometimes turquoise blue. Today it was both. With Barksee trotting alongside her, Kanani hummed and did some of the hand gestures she had learned at hula lessons. She loved it when they had the beach all to themselves. It was her own private paradise.

Suddenly Kanani stopped. They weren't alone after all. Kanani tightened her grip on Barksee's leash. In the distance, on the rocky side of the cove, something big and gray lay near the shore. Kanani squinted. Was it . . . ? Could it be . . . ? A monk seal!

Kanani remembered what the Monk Seal Foundation lady had told her class, and she knew what she was supposed to do. "Come on, Barksee!" she said, tugging his leash. Fortunately he hadn't seen the seal yet. "Let's go get help."

When Kanani neared the surf shack on Waipuna beach, she saw Celina and her brother waxing their surfboards. "Celina!" Kanani shouted. "There's a monk seal hauled out at 'Olino Cove! Seth, can you call the monk seal coordinators and ask them to send some volunteers?"

"You got it!" he said, heading inside.

"Wait!" Kanani called after him. "Here!" She handed him Barksee's leash, and then she and Celina took off for the cove.

"Where is it?" Celina asked as they scampered over the rocks to the small secluded beach.

"Over there!" Kanani pointed to the long gray shape that lay stretched out in the sand. As they drew near, they slowed down and both stared.

"I—I can't believe it," Kanani stammered, shaking her head.

Celina snorted. "That's your monk seal?"

Lying on the sand, with the waves gently washing over it, was a fat gray tree trunk.

Kanani's shoulders slumped. "I . . . I really thought it was a seal," she faltered. "I mean, there have been sightings nearby recently, and . . . well, I was just so sure."

"From far away it really looks like a seal," Celina consoled her. She put her arm around Kanani's shoulders. "We'd better get back and tell Seth so that he can let the monk seal people know it was a false alarm."

"I'm so embarrassed," Kanani moaned.

"Don't worry about it," Celina told her. "Actually, it was sort of nice coming down here, just the two of us. You know, without your cousin. I mean she's okay and everything, but I miss spending all day with you, like old times."

"Thanks for trying to cheer me up," Kanani said, offering Celina a weak smile.

That night, Kanani was as quiet as Rachel, who spent the evening with her nose buried in a book. Finally, Rachel looked up and asked, "Kanani, is everything all right? You're usually so talkative."

"I made a huge fuss over a tree trunk," Kanani said glumly. "I feel so stupid."

"You did what?"

Kanani hesitated before spilling out the whole story about the monk seal that wasn't. Surely Rachel would think she was an idiot!

But instead of laughing, Rachel said, "It was an honest mistake, and you were trying to do something good. I'm sure everyone understands."

"Do you really think so?" Kanani asked. "I mean, two volunteers showed up, and you should have seen their faces when they saw the tree trunk. They were so disappointed."

"Things aren't always what they appear to be, and sometimes it's easy to get confused," Rachel pointed out.

"Thanks," Kanani said. "I appreciate that."

Later, after Rachel had gone to bed, Kanani wrote in her diary,

Rachel didn't make fun of my monk seal mistake. Instead, she tried to comfort me. Maybe I'm the one who has misjudged her.

Call for Help

The next morning, when Kanani left to help in the store as usual, her cousin was still on the computer. Every day after breakfast, Rachel checked to see if there was an e-mail from her mother. On the days that she got one, Rachel was happy, and on days without an e-mail, she was even quieter than usual. On those days, Kanani felt at a loss. The more she tried to cheer her cousin up, the further Rachel seemed to retreat.

At Akina's, Kanani set about filling the candy jars. Just as she was filling one with chocolate-covered coffee beans, she heard Rachel ask, "Do you need any help?"

Kanani whipped around, spilling coffee beans everywhere. "Sure!" she answered, trying to hide her surprise. She hadn't expected to see Rachel at the store.

"Maybe I can start by helping you clean those up," Rachel said, smiling. "Where do you keep the broom?"

The rest of the morning, Kanani and Rachel worked side by side at the candy counter. At first they kept bumping into each other, but soon they slipped into a smooth rhythm. Rachel took the orders, and Kanani weighed and bagged the candies. Then they sent the guests over to Mrs. Akina at the cash register.

"You're both doing a marvelous job," Kanani's father noted. "By the way, Rachel, when you're done, help yourself to anything you want."

Kanani laughed when Rachel's eyes grew big. "It's one of the benefits of working at Akina's!" she told her cousin.

After lunch, Kanani went to find Barksee to take him for his walk. She slipped her camera into her pocket. Maybe today she'd be lucky and snap a photo of a rainbow or a sea turtle. When she stepped into the backyard, she spotted Mochi gnawing on a magazine and Barksee curled up on the lounge chair with Rachel, who was going through her collection of postcards.

"This one," Rachel explained to Barksee, "is from Paris. See, that's the Eiffel Tower. In France they let people take their dogs to restaurants." When Barksee wagged his tail, Rachel gave him a huge hug. "I wish I had a dog just like you," she said.

Kanani smiled. Barksee was a great listener.

"I'm going to take Barksee for his walk now. Want to come?" Kanani asked. She was already halfway across the yard when, to her surprise, Rachel said, "Sure, why not?"

After a short hike along the narrow, winding trail, Kanani helped Rachel up the rocks that led to the secret entrance of 'Olino Cove. "Here we are!" she announced proudly.

"This is so beautiful," Rachel whispered, even though no one else was around. "Look at how the water sparkles!"

It was true. The sun's reflection on the water made it look like diamonds sprinkled across a blanket of turquoise. "'*Olino* means 'sparkling' in Hawaiian," Kanani told her.

Rachel bent down and picked up a small black crab out of a tide pool. "Look!" she called to Kanani. "Should I keep it? Maybe I can put it in a jar."

Kanani shook her head. "It's probably not a great idea. Imagine what it would be like to be plucked from your home and carried away."

Rachel's face clouded over. "I would definitely hate that," she said. Gently, she returned the crab to the tide pool. Then she retreated to the shade of a palm tree and opened her black notebook. Kanani and Barksee sat down beside her.

"Why, those are pictures," Kanani said after sneaking a peek at Rachel's notebook. "You've been drawing!"

"What did you think I was doing?"

"I dunno. Writing, I guess. May I see?"

Rachel shook her head. "It's kind of personal." She went back to sketching. After a few minutes, she turned to Kanani. "How come you've never shown me 'Olino Cove before?"

"It's a secret that only locals know about," Kanani explained. "Too many tourists might ruin it."

A frown crossed Rachel's face. "Is that how you think of me—as a tourist?"

"I didn't mean *you!*" Kanani quickly said. "That came out all wrong. What I meant was—"

"I know what you meant," Rachel said stiffly. "I know you're forced to spend the month with me."

"That's not true!" Kanani protested.

Rachel bit her lip and looked away. "My mom didn't want me on her honeymoon, and my dad's too busy with his job right now, and you don't want me here either. You'd rather be alone at your precious beach than having to drag me around."

Kanani bristled. Rachel had no idea how hard she had been trying to make her feel welcome! "Well," she retorted, "you've made it very clear that you would rather be at an art museum or a ballet in New York than in this boring little town."

Call for Help

"Well, you act as if there's no place better than Waipuna," Rachel shot back. "You should hear yourself! 'We have the most beautiful beaches. We have our own waterfalls. We have—'"

"Me?" Kanani's voice rose. "What about you and all your 'New York has the best restaurants' and 'New York has the greatest museums'? Even your waterfalls are better. It must be torture for you to have to be here with a hick like me."

"I didn't have a choice," Rachel said. Her eyes were starting to tear up. "No one asked me what I wanted to do—"

Just then Barksee started barking, but both girls were too upset to pay attention to him. His barks became louder, and he strained at his leash. Finally, Rachel turned. "What's that?" she asked, pointing in the direction in which Barksee was straining.

Kanani squinted at a large, brownish-gray lump in the sand. She hesitated. "I—I think it's a monk seal," she stammered. "But it's so small . . ."

Quickly, she grabbed Barksee's leash and tied it to a palm tree so that he couldn't bother the seal—if it was a seal. It sure looked like one. The girls ran down the beach and stared. "It *is* a monk seal," Kanani said. "It looks very young, and it's all tangled up!" The seal had a net tightly wound around its body, and it wasn't moving.

"Shouldn't we try to get the net off?" Rachel asked anxiously.

Kanani shook her head. "No—we need to get help. Can you stay here while I go for help?"

"But what should I do?" Rachel's voice wavered. "Don't leave me!"

"Someone needs to make sure nobody bothers the seal. As soon as the word gets out, people will start showing up. Just tell them to keep away from the seal. I'll be back as soon as I call for help."

Rachel looked worried, but she nodded.

Kanani kicked off her flip-flops and raced along the trail toward the pier. Finally she spotted Pika near his father's boat.

"Oooh, look at the surfer girl run," Pika teased. "Don't wipe out!"

Kanani tried to catch her breath. "There's a monk seal on the beach at 'Olino Cove!" she gasped.

"Yeah, I've heard that one before," Pika laughed. "Like yesterday, when *someone* said they saw a monk seal and it was just an old tree trunk."

"This time it's real," Kanani insisted. "And it's in trouble!"

Pika's mischievous grin slid off his face. "For real?" he asked.

"Pika, I'm not going to make the same mistake twice!" Kanani ran on. There was no time to argue with him. She needed to get help, and fast.

Kanani ran past the beach and down the block, and then she was at Akina's. "Mom," she shouted as she ran into the store, "there's a monk seal stranded in 'Olino Cove. It's tangled in a net. We've got to call for help!"

Immediately, Mrs. Akina picked up the telephone. Kanani paced nearby, trying to overhear the conversation. "He wants to talk to you," her mother said, handing Kanani the phone.

"Kanani, this is Ron Lee. I'm the federal government monk seal coordinator for Kaua'i," a deep voice said. "Can you tell me, was the net wrapped around just part of the seal, or its entire body?"

"Its entire body," Kanani told him.

"Was the seal moving at all? Was it alive?"

"It was alive," she said, "but it wasn't moving. I saw the seal's eyes, and it blinked at me."

"Do you know how long it has been there?"

"No," Kanani said, wishing she could be more helpful.

"Okay, this sounds pretty serious," Ron told her. "I'm going to call a marine biologist, but it'll take her about an hour to get there. I'm also going to call a volunteer from the Monk Seal Foundation to get up there. Meanwhile, I need your help."

Kanani's breath quickened "What do you want me to do?"

"Go back to the cove and keep an eye on the seal. I want you to monitor it until help arrives. Make sure that people keep their distance and move up by the trees, off the beach. And no loud noises. We don't want the seal to panic. Can you do that?"

"I'll do my best," Kanani told him.

By the time Kanani made it back to the cove, a small crowd had gathered. Kanani spotted Pika and his friends, along with a few tourists.

"Help is coming," she called. Her heart was beating so fast, it felt as if it was going to fall out. "Everyone, please stay back." Kanani turned to her cousin. "How's the seal doing?"

Rachel shook her head. She looked panicky. "It doesn't look good. I think the net might be suffocating it."

Kanani felt sick at the thought of the seal pup suffocating. Even from a distance, the seal's huge

66

brown eyes looked so helpless. She felt the same way. Kanani noticed that Rachel was blinking back tears.

"Are you all right?" she asked.

Rachel wiped her eyes with the back of her hand. "That poor baby seal is probably so scared."

Kanani reached for Rachel's hand and squeezed it. "We're doing everything we can to help." She faced the curious people who were gathered around and inching closer. "Please give the seal more space!" she called.

"Who put you in charge?" Pika demanded.

"The coordinator from the federal government," Kanani answered. "Now stop bothering me. I have work to do."

"Yes, sir," Pika said sarcastically.

"Please stay back, away from the seal," Kanani called again, careful not to be too loud.

Pika shook his head. "Sheesh, do I have to do everything? You need to sound like you're in charge, like this: Listen up, people—give the seal some space!"

For a small boy, he made a big impression. Kanani couldn't help but smile as Pika cleared the beach. He started to smile back but then caught himself and scowled at her instead.

It seemed to take forever for the biologist to

arrive. Rachel and Pika helped keep the crowd back while Kanani took photos and monitored the seal. Every now and then it made a low barking sound that sounded like a desperate cry for help. Kanani knew that seals could overheat in the sun. How long had it been out of the water, trapped in the net? Was it badly injured? She wished the biologist would hurry!

In the distance, Kanani saw a tall man wearing a monk seal T-shirt sprinting toward them. He had an official-looking nametag around his neck. Kanani waved and went to meet him.

"Kanani? I'm Jim Robins, a volunteer from the Hawaiian Monk Seal Foundation. Mahalo for your quick help," he said as he slowly approached the seal. His face lost color when he saw how tightly the net was wrapped around the seal.

As Jim roped off the area, Mrs. Akina came running. Close behind her was a woman with short brown hair carrying a metal box.

"That's Dr. Julia Anderson. She's a terrific marine biologist," Jim told Kanani as Julia ducked under the rope and cautiously approached the seal from behind. Her face remained serious as she waved Jim over to assist her.

Mrs. Akina came up to her daughter. "Where's Rachel?" she asked.

Kanani had completely forgotten about her cousin. She looked around but couldn't see her anywhere. Finally she glanced toward the lava rocks, and there, sitting away from the crowd, was Rachel. She was hugging Barksee.

Kanani ran over to her. "Are you okay?"

Rachel shrugged. "Is the baby seal going to be all right?" she asked in a shaky voice.

"We'll know soon," Kanani said. "Let's go see."

Rachel shook her head. "You go. I'll stay with Barksee."

Kanani held her breath as the biologist set about removing the net. Jim had a firm hold of the seal's neck. Julia took a pair of shears from the tool box. No one dared move or speak as she slowly began to cut the net. Kanani's eyes filled with tears of relief as the net fell away and the seal began to wriggle.

Jim continued holding its head while Julia put orange tags on the seal's rear flippers. Then she picked up the box and equipment and moved outside the ropes. Jim released the seal's head and quickly stepped back to join Julia. A huge cheer went up from the crowd as the seal moved swiftly into the water.

Call for Help

"Kanani," said Julia, wiping her brow, "thank you for your help. I heard you were the one who first spotted the seal."

"Yes, me and my cousin," Kanani told her.

"I helped, too!" Pika added.

Jim smiled. "Mahalo to all of you."

"What's going to happen to the seal?" Kanani asked.

"She has injuries where the net cut her," Julia said, "but because we got here so soon—thanks to your quick action—her cuts aren't life threatening. She'll scar, but G-68 is one tough little seal."

"G-68?" Kanani asked.

"That's what we'll call her," Julia explained. "I tagged her so that we can identify her whenever she's sighted. I recognize most of the monk seals on Kaua'i, but this one's new to me. She's probably only about four months old."

"I was pretty sure she was a pup," Kanani said.

"You were right," said Julia.

"She's so cute!" Kanani said. "But G-68 sounds like—well, like a name of a robot or something. Would it be okay if I give her a nickname?"

"Of course," Julia said. "After all, you helped save her."

Kanani thought for a moment. "How about Malana?" Kanani said. "In Hawaiian, that means 'floating,' or 'one who floats.'"

Julia smiled. "That's perfect for a seal!"

As the crowd began to break up, a young man wearing glasses hurried toward them. "Hello! I'm David Fong with the *Daily Breeze*. Kanani Akina? Everyone says I should talk to you. You discovered the monk seal first?"

"Well, not just me, but my cousin Rachel, too," Kanani told him.

"Where is Rachel?" asked Mr. Fong.

"She's over there," Kanani said, turning around and looking toward the rocks. But Rachel was gone.

When Kanani got home, she found Rachel sitting in the yard under the mango tree. Jinx was strutting back and forth, trying to get her attention, but Rachel ignored him.

"Where were you?" Kanani asked as she set her camera down. "There was a newspaper reporter who wanted to interview you. He even wants to use some of my photos. Isn't it exciting? Think about it: we helped save a Hawaiian monk seal!"

Call for Help

Rachel looked away. "I was so worried. As soon as I saw the seal go back to the water, I left." Her eyes were red, as if she had been crying.

"There's nothing to be worried about any more," Kanani assured her. "Jim and Dr. Anderson said she's going to be okay."

"Yes, but she's just a baby and she's all alone," Rachel said. "What if she needs help again and no one is there?"

"Dr. Anderson says she's very tough," Kanani noted, but nothing she could say eased Rachel's fears.

Later that evening, Kanani wrote,

Dear Diary,

Just when Rachel and I were finally getting along, we had a fight at 'Olino Cove. Then together we helped rescue a seal pup. Yes, a monk seal! But here's the weird part: instead of being happy about it, Rachel seems sad. And the more I talked about it, the sadder she got. Then finally she broke down crying.

What's wrong with me? Instead of making Rachel feel good, all I seem to do is make her miserable.

Everyone cheered when Kanani walked into Akina's the next morning. "Look, it's the girl who helped rescue the monk seal!" a customer called out.

As Kanani blushed, her mother rushed up with a copy of the *Daily Breeze*. "Kanani, the seal story made the front page, and they used your photos!"

Kanani gasped. Sure enough, next to an article about the rescue was a photo she had taken of Julia freeing the monk seal from the net. There was another photo of Pika waving his arms and ordering people to stay back, and one of Malana slipping into the sea. Beside each photo a caption read, "Photo courtesy of Kanani Akina."

"May I have your autograph?" asked Aunty Lea.

"I want one, too," Aunty Aimee added.

"Who wants *my* autograph? That's me in the paper," Pika announced as he burst into the store. "Only I look more handsome in person."

After the crowd had left, Pika lingered. "Hey, where's your cousin?" he asked Kanani. "Has she seen my picture?"

"She's at my house," Kanani told him.

"Why?" asked Pika, chewing on the gummy frogs he had bought. "What did you do to her?"

Kanani felt a prickle of annoyance. "I didn't do

anything to her. She just wants some time alone."

"Yeah, okay, right. Whatever," he said, not sounding convinced.

Kanani reminded herself that Pika was simply trying to provoke. After all, he was possibly the most annoying person on the planet. Yet she wondered, was Rachel still angry with her? What could she do to make her cousin feel better?

"Well, I'd love to stand around and chat," Pika said, "but my surfboard awaits."

Stand around—suddenly Kanani thought of something. Whenever she was upset or sad, the ocean always cheered her up. If she could just find a way to get Rachel in—or on—the water, maybe it would work for her, too . . .

"Mahalo, Pika!," Kanani said.

Pika frowned at her. "Mahalo for what?"

"For giving me a great idea!"

"I don't know," Rachel said as she stroked Barksee. "I'm not too keen on surprises."

"I really think you're going to like this one," Kanani assured her.

Rachel hesitated. "What do I have to do?"

"Just put on some swimwear, and follow me."

At the surf shack, a couple of older girls were flirting with Seth.

"Ahem!" Kanani coughed into her hand.

Seth turned. "Hey, Kanani, what's up?"

"We'd like to rent those," Kanani said, pointing at two longboards. "With paddles."

As Seth went to fetch the boards, Rachel paled. "I can't surf, Kanani, you know that! I thought we were going to see tide pools or something safe like that."

"These are paddleboards," Kanani explained. "You don't have to swim and you don't even have to get in the water, but you can still see how wonderful it is being out on the ocean!"

"I don't know . . ." Rachel looked skeptical.

"You told me that you've been in a rowboat in Central Park, right?" Rachel nodded. "This is sort of like that, only a lot more fun. Just try it for ten minutes. If you hate it, we'll come right back, I promise."

"Okay, ten minutes," Rachel said, sounding reluctant. "Ten minutes, and then we come in."

Seth returned with two boards about twice as tall as Kanani and Rachel. "A stand-up paddleboard is bigger than a surfboard, and you can just sit on it—you don't have to stand if you don't want to," he explained to Rachel. "Plus, there's a paddle to help you get around. Come on, I'll give you a lesson."

Rachel paid close attention to everything Seth said. After practicing with the boards in the sand, the girls were ready for the water. "Here, put these on," said Seth, handing them each a life jacket.

Kanani went first, wading up to her hips while Rachel watched from the shore. Kanani eased herself onto the board and then kneeled. "Look," she called to Rachel. "I'm not even getting wet! I'm just sitting here."

"It doesn't look too hard," Rachel said warily.

"I'll be keeping an eye on you two," Seth assured her. "Don't worry. We'll stay close to the shore where the water is shallow."

As Rachel walked toward the water, Kanani stood up on her board. With no waves to worry about, she felt in control. "Come on, Rachel," she called. "I'll be with you the whole time. You won't be alone."

Cautiously, Rachel placed her board in the water. Seth held it steady as she got on it and sat up.

Kanani paddled over. "The ocean is amazing," she told Rachel. "I've been wanting to share it with you since you first arrived. When you're out here, it's as if all your worries are washed away. It's just you and the sea."

Seth followed at a distance as the girls paddled away from the shore. First Rachel kneeled. After a while, she cautiously stood up and balanced on her board like her cousin.

"You did it!" Kanani shouted. "See? You're up!"

"Look at me!" Rachel exclaimed as she pushed forward with her paddle.

"Oh dear," Kanani said, looking troubled.

"What?" Rachel asked. "Is something wrong?"

"Well, it's been over ten minutes," Kanani said. "I guess you're going to want to quit now."

Rachel laughed. "No way—I could do this for ten hours!"

"You should have seen her," Kanani boasted to her mother. "She was a natural out on the water!"

Mrs. Akina was driving Rachel and Kanani to the Monk Seal Foundation office.

Rachel blushed. "You were right—it was amazing, and I wasn't even scared. Well, maybe a little at first," Rachel confessed. "But paddleboarding is really fun, and a lot easier than I expected."

"She has great balance because of all her ballet training," Kanani told her mom. "I had to force her to

78

come in. At the very end she was even swimming! We're going back in the water tomorrow."

"And every day after that," Rachel added.

Mrs. Akina laughed as she pulled into the parking lot. "It looks like we have another mermaid in the family!"

When they saw the Monk Seal Foundation sign, both girls began talking at once.

"I hope Malana's okay."

"I wonder if she'll ever return to Waipuna?"

"Do you think she'd remember us if she saw us again?"

Jim was waiting in the lobby. "Aloha, ladies. Welcome to the world headquarters of the Hawaiian Monk Seal Foundation." The small office was cramped, and every bit of wall space was devoted to photos and information about Hawaiian monk seals.

"So, you've come for an update on G-68, also known as Malana? Well, I'm happy to report that she was sighted this morning near Waipuna Beach."

"Is she back with her mother?" Rachel asked.

Jim pointed to a poster. "Malana is about four months old, like this one here. When monk seal pups are about six weeks old, they stop nursing, and their mothers leave them to fend for themselves."

Rachel gulped. "But she's just a baby!"

"To us it may seem young, but the pups are ready to be on their own. Still, they are vulnerable. That's why we monitor them and get help if there's trouble. With only about twelve hundred Hawaiian monk seals left, every pup is critically important." As Jim talked, Kanani noticed that Rachel had gone quiet. "Pups and adults must haul out to rest," he went on. "So if you see a monk seal on the shore, keep your distance. It's for their safety, and yours."

On the ride home, Kanani was eager to brainstorm ideas. "We need to make people at the beach more aware, so they know to keep away when a seal hauls out. Maybe we could get the newspaper to write more articles . . ." But instead of chiming in, Rachel just stared out the window. Finally, Kanani gave up and just stared out the window, too.

That night Kanani asked her diary,

How can I help an endangered species, when I can't even help my own cousin? Something's not right, but I can't seem to break through to her. I can sense that she's sad, but she won't tell me why—and that makes me sad, too.

With less than a week left of Rachel's visit, the girls had fallen into a comfortable routine: helping at Akina's in the mornings, and afternoons at the beach. Rachel seemed happiest when she was out on the water. Kanani understood this and felt pleased that she had found a way to lift her cousin's spirits. And yet Kanani still sensed an undertow of sadness. She ached to connect with Rachel and learn what was troubling her, but she didn't know how to reach her, and Rachel kept her thoughts and feelings to herself.

One afternoon, as the lifeguard looked on, the girls paddled out past the wave break. The sea foam lining the shore resembled a white ribbon wrapping up the beach like a present.

"I'm going to miss Hawai'i," Rachel said wistfully.

"Really?" Kanani was pleased—but surprised.

"Definitely," Rachel sighed. "I feel like I really know this whole place. It almost feels like home now."

Kanani smiled. "There is one place that you haven't seen yet."

Rachel raised her eyebrows. "Really? I thought I had seen everything in Waipuna."

"Nope, you haven't seen the most beautiful spot of all," said Kanani mysteriously.

"I haven't?" Rachel asked. "Will you show me?"

"Yes—we'll go tomorrow! But first I need to set things up. Come on, let's go find Pika."

"Pika?! Why *him*, of all people?" Now Rachel was really puzzled.

Kanani grinned. "You'll find out tomorrow.

As the girls walked home through town, they spotted Tutu Lani sitting on a bench fanning herself.

"Aloha, keiki!" she said. "Rachel, how are you?"

Rachel considered. "I think I'm happy and sad," she answered. "Happy because I'm going to see my mom soon, but sad because that means I'll be leaving. Everyone here has been so nice."

Tutu Lani smiled. "Here in Waipuna, we try hard to make our visitors feel like *'ohana*—like family. But don't worry, you'll be able to take all your fond memories with you." Tutu Lani pressed her hands against her heart. "This is where I keep mine, and I am proud to say that my heart is full. Now, would you two young ladies mind assisting an old lady?"

"We'd love to," Kanani said. The girls helped the elderly woman up. Each took one of her arms, and together they walked Tutu Lani home.

The next afternoon, Kanani and Rachel headed down Waipuna Beach toward the dock. In the water was a gleaming white catamaran with *Pika's Paradise* in fancy black lettering along the side.

"We sail to this mysterious place?" Rachel asked.

Kanani's eyes twinkled mischievously. "That's right."

Pika came out on the deck. "This is my dad's boat," he boasted to Rachel as he munched on a handful of rice crackers. "He's going to be your captain."

Pika's father waved from the helm.

"Are you coming too?" Rachel asked Pika.

"I don't know," Pika said, looking bored. "I'm a pretty busy person. Well, since you're forcing me to, I guess I have no choice."

"Nobody's forcing you," Kanani pointed out.

"Fine! Yes! Okay, I'll go," Pika said, raising his voice. "You don't have to be so pushy."

As the catamaran set sail, Kanani closed her eyes and enjoyed the cool spray of the ocean against her skin. After a short time, Waipuna and the other small towns that lined the coast gave way to majestic cliffs and deep canyons blanketed with velvety green.

Silver waterfalls cascaded down the emerald cliffs of the Na Pali Coast and into the ocean.

Suddenly, Rachel grabbed Kanani's arm and yelled, "Look! Over there!"

Kanani turned as a pod of dolphins leaped in and out of the water. The catamaran slowed to a stop as the dolphins swam near the boat as if to greet the passengers. Dolphins were a common sight around Waipuna, but Kanani never tired of seeing them.

"Thank you, Kanani," Rachel said. Her eyes shone. "This is amazing. I'll always remember this."

"We're not done," Kanani said. "You haven't seen the special place yet."

Rachel looked at her cousin with disbelief. "You mean, there's *more?*"

Kanani grinned. "Just wait till you see it—it's magical!"

After a little while, Pika's father pulled in the sail. He handed Rachel a snorkel vest and showed her how to put it on, along with her flippers and mask. "I'm not so sure about this," Rachel said warily. "What if the fish try to eat me?"

"Sheesh," Pika said. "Don't be coconut brain! What fish would want to eat *you?*" Before Rachel could reply, Pika was in the water.

Rachel looked apprehensive.

"The vest will keep you afloat," Kanani assured her. "You wanted to see the most beautiful spot in Hawaii? Well, it's right here . . . beneath us."

Rachel took a deep breath. "Well, what are we waiting for?" she said and pulled on her mask.

As Kanani lowered herself into the water, she could feel her body relax and her heart lift. Shafts of sunlight lit up a watery blue-green world. Schools of reef fish swam slowly past—orange angelfish, yellow butterfly fish, blue-striped snapper. Their vivid hues were so dazzling that it was like swimming through a rainbow. When a group of gray and black triggerfish went by, Kanani tapped Rachel on the shoulder. The girls lifted their heads and removed their snorkels.

"Is everything okay?" Rachel asked.

Kanani nodded. "Did you see all those gray and black fish? Those are the humuhumunukunukua-pua'a. Our state fish!"

"Humu-huma-whatta?" Rachel sputtered.

Kanani laughed. "Humu-humu-nuku-nuku-apu-a-a," she said. "I'll teach you how to say it later. How's the snorkeling?"

"Amazingly awesome!" Rachel said and pulled her mask back on before Kanani could reply.

A Magical Place

Kanani adjusted her mask and continued snorkeling again. Suddenly she spotted something large and dark green in the distance. A sea turtle! Quickly, she swam to Rachel, but by the time she reached her, the turtle was gone.

Later, back in the catamaran, Kanani told her cousin, "I was hoping you'd see the turtle. They're considered good luck."

Rachel let out a contented sigh. "I already feel lucky to have seen all that I did," she said. "It was just as you said it would be—magical. Thank you for bringing me here."

"Hey," Pika chimed in, "what about me? It's *Pika's Paradise* that brought you here!"

Rachel laughed. "Thank you, Pika!"

The next afternoon the weather was cloudy, so the girls took a break from swimming. Kanani chased Mochi around the yard, while Rachel stretched out on the lounge chair and sketched in her black notebook. Kanani tried to pretend she wasn't interested in Rachel's sketchbook, but finally she couldn't stand it any longer.

"Can I *pleeease* see what you're drawing?" she asked.

"It's only doodles," Rachel said, holding her sketchbook against her chest. "Nothing major."

"Please, Rachel?" Kanani begged. "I showed you the most magical place in Hawai'i—you can at least show me your sketchbook!"

"Well, okay, I guess so," Rachel said. "If you really want to see it." She handed over the black notebook and watched silently as Kanani examined it page by page.

It was all there: Akina's, the lu'au, 'Olino Cove, Barksee, Malana, Waipuna Kitchen, and even Tutu Lani. Kanani turned back to the drawing of herself hula-dancing onstage with a radiant smile.

"I really admired the way you could dance in front of all those people at the lu'au," Rachel said, peering over her shoulder. "I could never be that brave."

"Oh, but you are," Kanani insisted. "You came all the way from New York to Hawai'i by yourself. You stayed with Malana even when you didn't want to be alone. You swam in the ocean even though you were afraid, and you've paddleboarded and snorkeled."

Rachel reached down to pat Barksee. "I guess I did do all that!"

Kanani turned back to the notebook. "Rachel, you're a true artist."

"They're just little sketches," Rachel replied, sounding pleased.

"No, really, these are terrific," Kanani said as she admired a picture of a tide pool. "Hey, why don't we go to the cove? You can sketch there, and I'll bring my camera."

On their way to the cove, the girls stopped at Akina's. "We just got a special delivery," Mr. Akina said, beaming. "Come check it out—our new portable shave-ice cart!" He led the girls behind the store and pointed proudly to a bright pink cart with a thatched roof. There were places for syrups and spoons, and a white board to write the flavors on. "Akina's Shave Ice —Sorta Famous" was painted on the front.

"Wow, Dad—I love it," said Kanani. "What are you going to do with it?"

"We'll put it down by the pier during the Arts and Crafts Festival next month," he replied. "Now, I expect that you girls stopped in for a reason. What flavors would you like?"

"Do you have apple?" Rachel asked.

"We have over fifty flavors—but no apple!" Mr. Akina said with a laugh. "We do have pine-apple. It's not the same, but it sure tastes good."

Kanani ordered coconut and passion fruit, and

Rachel had pineapple and raspberry. The girls took their time strolling through town, stopping to say hello to everyone they ran into. Finally, they climbed the rocks and stepped into the cove—and stopped and stared. A small crowd had gathered, and there, a short distance away, a young monk seal lay hauled out on the wet sand.

Kanani hurried over. "Please, everyone," she called out, "stand back and give the seal more space."

A boy laughed. "Yeah, says you and who else?"

"You heard her; stand back!"

Kanani whipped around in surprise. It was Rachel, with a fierce scowl. The boy quickly took a few steps back. "Farther," said Kanani, glaring at him. Then she turned and exchanged a grin with Rachel.

"It's Malana, isn't it?" Rachel whispered. She took out a pencil and opened her sketchbook.

"I'm pretty sure it is," Kanani agreed. "Look, there are the scars where her cuts healed up."

The girls looked at Malana resting peacefully on the sand. She seemed at home in 'Olino Cove.

"Well," Kanani said, "I guess we'd better alert the volunteers and let them know that there's a healthy young monk seal here in Waipuna!"

That evening Kanani was eager to write in her diary. Malana had returned! But as she entered her room and was going to her dresser, she spotted something green peeking out from beneath Rachel's pillow. It looked like . . . like the corner of her diary.

Could it be? Kanani hesitated. No, it wasn't possible—surely Rachel wouldn't have taken her diary. Would she?

Her heart pounding, Kanani lifted the pillow.

It *was* her diary.

She sat on the bed, feeling as if she couldn't breathe. After everything she and Rachel had done together, this was how Rachel thanked her?

Kanani opened the book, and her heart lurched. Rachel had not only stolen her diary, she had written all over the pages!

"Dear Diary, I know I'm supposed to be happy that Mom got married again. But instead, I feel abandoned," one passage said.

Kanani flipped to another page. "Mom says she's having a great time on her honeymoon. What if she and Paul decide they don't want me living with them now that they're married?"

On another page, Rachel had written, "My life has been turned upside down. Sometimes I cry myself to *sleep. I have to be quiet since I'm sharing Kanani's room and I don't want to wake her—"*

"WHAT ARE YOU DOING?" Rachel screamed.

Startled, Kanani jerked her head up. The diary fell out of her hands. A photo of Rachel and her mother tumbled out, along with a couple of postcards. Swiftly, Rachel picked up the things on the floor. "I can't believe you were reading my diary!" she said, her voice quivering.

Kanani shook her head to try to clear it. "*Your* diary? But this is *my* diary!"

"It's mine!" Rachel's eyes flashed with anger. "I had it hidden under my pillow, and you took it!"

Suddenly, color came back to Kanani's face. "Oh no!" she gasped. She ran to her dresser. There, buried beneath her T-shirts, was her diary, right where she always kept it. "Oh, Rachel, I think I know what happened. We have the same diary! I mistook yours for mine," she said in a rush, holding up the green book. "Look—they're exactly the same!"

Now it was Rachel's turn to be confused. "The same diary?"

Slowly, the answer began to dawn on Kanani. "Where did you get yours?"

"Grandma sent it to me for Christmas."

"Me too," Kanani exclaimed. "Grandma must have bought us the same gift! Just like she gave us the exact same dresses at the family reunion—"

"—and we both have the same alarm clock," Rachel added. "But Kanani, why were you snooping around? My diary was hidden under my pillow."

"It was sticking out," Kanani insisted. "I thought that it was mine and that you had taken it. I wasn't snooping—honest!"

"You thought I stole your diary?" Rachel looked insulted.

"Well, what was I supposed to think? It looked like *my* diary under *your* pillow. Besides, you thought I stole yours," Kanani pointed out.

"I guess that's true," Rachel conceded. The anger faded from her face, and sudden tears shimmered in her eyes. "But—how much did you read?"

"Not too much," Kanani stammered. "Hardly any."

Rachel looked relieved. "There's nothing important in there anyway," she said, holding it tightly. "Just a bunch of doodles and stuff. It's no big deal."

"Right, it's no big deal," Kanani echoed. She climbed onto her futon, relieved that they hadn't ended up in a fight. Yet, as she lay there, trying to fall asleep,

Kanani couldn't stop thinking about the things her cousin had written.

The next morning, the girls got up late and hurried to Akina's. Rachel seemed to be her normal quiet self, but Kanani still felt uneasy about the diary episode from the night before.

"You two are awfully quiet today," said Mrs. Akina. "Here comes Aunty Lea. Maybe she'll liven things up around here."

Aunty Lea let out a whoop when Kanani and Rachel pronounced her chocolate chip banana bread ono-licious. "The bananas are from Tutu Lani's garden," she said. "I promised her a couple of loaves."

"I'll take them to her," Kanani volunteered. "If that's all right with you," she asked her mother.

"Thank you, Kanani—that would save me a long walk," Aunty Lea said.

"Go on then," her mother told her. "Rachel and I will try to keep the store running without you."

"Aloha, Kanani!" Tutu Lani called out from her rocking chair.

"Aloha," Kanani called back. "I brought you something from Aunty Lea."

When Kanani handed over the banana bread, Tutu Lani's face lit up. But when she met Kanani's eyes, her smile faded. "What's troubling you, keiki?"

Kanani sat on the porch steps. "I'm fine," she began, but then she stopped herself and sighed. There was no point in trying to fool Tutu Lani. "I know it was wrong of me," Kanani confessed, "but I read parts of Rachel's diary. I didn't mean to—our diaries look exactly alike and I thought it was mine—but I can't stop thinking about what she wrote."

"Go on," Tutu Lani said gently.

"Her diary was full of pages about her mom," Kanani continued. "I knew Rachel missed her, but I had no idea how upset she feels about her mom getting remarried. I mean, she hardly ever mentions her."

"Silence can say a lot," Tutu Lani noted.

"What should I do?" Kanani asked.

"Try listening—even to the silence," Tutu Lani advised. "Perhaps it's time for *ho'opono*."

"Ho'opono?"

"That's when you do the right and honorable thing," Tutu Lani explained. "It's correcting your wrongs and moving on."

Kanani nodded slowly. "You're right," she said. "It is time for ho'opono."

Walking home, Kanani practiced what she wanted to say to Rachel, but nothing sounded right. Tutu Lani made it sound simple, but Kanani knew it wouldn't be easy. Every time she imagined telling Rachel what she had read in the diary, Kanani's heart pounded and her knees felt weak. What would Rachel think? What would she say?

Kanani felt as if she were marching to her doom. It was an oddly familiar feeling. Where had she felt such waves of panic before? Suddenly it came to her—facing the surf break, trying to stand up and ride a wave, only to be tossed helplessly in the frothing surf.

At home, Kanani found Rachel in the yard with Barksee. Kanani scooped up her dog for reassurance, took a deep breath, and said the words she had practiced: "Rachel, I have a confession to make. I did read some of your diary. It started as an accident, but that doesn't make it right. I am sorry—I really am. It was wrong of me."

Rachel tensed and turned her back to Kanani. "How much did you read?" she asked in a quiet voice.

Kanani hesitated. "More than I should have," she admitted. There was a knot in her stomach that was making it hard to breathe.

Suddenly she had an idea. "Why don't we go to 'Olino Cove? It might make both of us feel better."

At the cove, the girls sat on the lava rocks not far from where they had first spotted Malana. A long silence separated the cousins. Over and over, Rachel scooped up sand and let it run through her fingers. At first this made Kanani squirm, but after a while the flowing sand, like the rhythm of the waves, was soothing and hypnotic.

Suddenly Rachel spoke. "I know I'm supposed to be happy for my mom," she began. Her voice was so soft that Kanani strained to hear it over the sound of the ocean. "Her new husband, Paul, is a nice man. He really loves her, and he has always been kind to me. But I've never been so far away from my mother and for so long."

Kanani started to say something but stopped herself.

"I really miss her. I hope that she misses me, too," Rachel continued. "But I can't help worrying that she's too swept up with Paul to think about me." She picked up a stick and began drawing circles in the sand.

"I bet she thinks about you all the time,"
Kanani said. "Doesn't she e-mail you almost every day?"

Rachel nodded. "That's true, but—well, it's just
that everything is changing. I used to spend summers
with my father. But he just started a new job, and my
stepmom just had a new baby, and they felt it would
be too difficult for me to stay with them this summer.
So . . . here I am." Rachel tossed the stick away. "When
I get back I'll be living in a new place and going to a
new school, and Paul will be there, too. It will be like
starting a whole new life. A different life." She paused.

Kanani listened to the silence.

Rachel spoke again. "It's been just my mom and
me for such a long time. I liked things the way they
were. I was happy." Her voice shook. "And what if
Paul doesn't want me? What will happen then? Where
will I go?"

Kanani put her arm around her cousin. When
she felt her trembling, she hugged her tighter. "Oh,
Rachel, those are a lot of big changes and new things in
your life." It was all clear now—why Rachel had looked
tense and unhappy when she first arrived, why she so
often looked troubled. "But I'm positive both of your
parents love you very much and want you."

Rachel let go of a deep breath. "Mom did say

that if I didn't want her to marry Paul, she wouldn't."

"Why did you tell her it was okay?" Kanani asked.

"Because I want her to be happy," said Rachel.

"Is she happy when she's with him?"

"Yes," Rachel nodded. "She's really happy. Happier than I've ever seen her."

There was another long silence. But this one felt comfortable. Kanani looked at her cousin and realized how close she felt to her. It was a deep, joyful, happy feeling—sort of like diving into a calm, clear ocean for a relaxing swim.

"You know what, Kanani?"

"What?"

A small smile crept across Rachel's face. "I'm sort of glad you read my diary."

Kanani caught her breath. "You are?"

"Yes. I feel much better now. I don't feel so scared about everything. Somehow, talking about it with you makes it easier to imagine that things are going to be okay. Thank you for listening. And for understanding."

Kanani smiled back. "I think the real thanks go to Grandma for sending us the same diary. Here's to you and me, and to Grandma!" *And to Tutu Lani,* she thought, *for teaching me about ho'opono.*

Suddenly Kanani grinned and caught Rachel's eye. Raising her hand, she made a fist with her thumb and pinky extended and gave it a little shake.

"What's that?" Rachel asked.

"It's the *shaka* sign. Surfers use it. It means don't worry, everything's cool."

Rachel grinned and returned the shaka sign to her cousin.

As the last customers left Akina's with bags of sweets in their hands and smiles on their faces, Kanani said cheerfully, "Thank you for coming—we hope to see you again!"

Mr. Akina locked the front door, and Mrs. Akina began to wipe down the counters. "I know this is your last night, but I'm afraid we have to go out," Mr. Akina said to Rachel.

"Yes," Kanani's mother added. "We have plans for tonight that we just can't break."

"That's okay," Rachel said. "I understand."

"Don't worry about us," Kanani added. She tried to suppress a grin. "We can have fun on our own."

"Oh, wait," Mr. Akina said. He handed Rachel a package. "This is for you from all of us. Only you can't keep it."

Rachel looked puzzled as she unwrapped the gift. "Rachel's Big Apple?" she said, reading the words painted on a piece of driftwood.

"It's our newest shave-ice flavor!" Kanani announced. "We're putting it right up on the top of the board, so you'll always be here."

"Wow," Rachel said, beaming. "No one's ever named something after me before!"

"Would you like to try your new flavor before

I shut the machine down for the day?" Mr. Akina asked.

"Yes, please!" Rachel replied.

An hour later, Kanani and Rachel headed down Koa Street together for the last time. The sky was washed with tints of coral, gold, and sapphire. "Since my parents are going out to dinner," Kanani said, "we're supposed to eat at the Waipuna Kitchen tonight. Celina said her mom will be making something special for your last meal there."

"I hope it's saimin," Rachel said.

"I think it's a big bowl of poi," Kanani teased.

The restaurant was packed. When the girls entered, all at once the talking stopped.

"Look, there's Aunty Aimee and Aunty Lea," Rachel said, giving them a wave.

"Pika's over there with his parents," Kanani pointed out.

"Hey, there's Jim from the Monk Seal Foundation," said Rachel. "What's he doing here?"

"Aloha, Rachel," Tutu Lani called out.

"Aloha, Rachel," the rest of the guests repeated.

Rachel blinked. "Hey—I know everyone here tonight! How weird is that? What's going on?"

Kanani's eyes sparkled. "This is your good-bye

party! We're all going to miss you. We want you to think of Waipuna as your second home."

Just then Kanani's parents came in from the kitchen. "Was she surprised?" Mrs. Akina asked in a whisper, her eyes sparkling with delight.

"Just look," Kanani said with a laugh.

Rachel was still standing frozen with her mouth open. As she struggled for words, Tutu Lani came forward and placed a beautiful orchid lei around her neck. "Now you are 'ohana—part of our family here in Waipuna," Tutu Lani murmured as she folded Rachel into a hug.

When they got home that night, Rachel started packing. Kanani sat cross-legged on the floor and watched as the suitcases began to fill up. "Would you mind getting my sketchbook for me?" Rachel asked Kanani. "It's in the backyard on the table."

Under the full moon, the mango tree cast a long shadow. Kanani checked the picnic table, but the sketchbook wasn't there. As she was looking around the lounge chair, Mochi trotted by. As usual, something was hanging out of her mouth.

"Mochi!" Kanani scolded in horror as she

pried the sketchbook from the goat's mouth. "Oh, Mochi, how could you do this?"

Mochi strolled away, unconcerned.

"Did you find it?" Rachel asked as Kanani returned to the bedroom.

"Um . . . sort of." She held up the book. "Mochi did this." The sketchbook was seriously shredded.

Rachel's eyes grew wide, and Kanani felt her heart drop. An entire month of drawings—destroyed. Suddenly Rachel gasped. Was she crying? But when Kanani looked at Rachel, she was chuckling.

"Mochi left me something to always remember this summer by," Rachel said with a laugh. "And I gave her a good meal."

"But your drawings, your beautiful drawings," Kanani stammered. "Most of them are ruined!"

Rachel thumbed through what was left of the book. "There are still plenty of sketches left. And anyway, as Tutu Lani says, my fondest memories are here," she said, placing her hands over her heart.

That night the girls stayed up late and talked and talked while Barksee slept soundly on the bed. "You're so lucky," Rachel mused. "You have every-thing—your family and a town where everyone knows you. Akina's hasn't changed in years, and you're living in a tropical paradise."

"Do you really think so? I thought you didn't like it here," Kanani said. "I mean, compared to New York."

"I was just trying to impress you," Rachel admitted. "After all, you kept saying how great Waipuna is."

Kanani laughed. "*I* was trying to impress *you*! New York sounds so exciting, I was afraid that Waipuna wouldn't even begin to compare."

"You'll have to come visit me sometime," Rachel said. "It's totally different, with sidewalks everywhere and people rushing around. But it is exciting."

"I'd love to visit New York," Kanani said, adding with a sly grin, "I've already heard so much about it."

"Will you e-mail me?" Rachel asked.

"Of course," Kanani replied, "if you'll e-mail me back."

"Let's send each other postcards, too," Rachel suggested. "That way I can show you my favorite places at home, and you can remind me of Hawai'i."

Suddenly, Kanani remembered something. She went to her dresser. "This is for you," she said, handing Rachel the puka-shell bracelet.

"I love it," Rachel said. "Thank you. I mean, mahalo."

"I made it—that's why it looks lopsided," Kanani admitted.

"It's beautiful," Rachel said, slipping it on. "And it's even more special now that I know you made it."

Mrs. Akina stepped into the girls' room. "Lights out, ladies. It's almost midnight! Good night, Rachel. Good night, Kanani." Just as she turned out the lights, a loud crowing could be heard outside the window.

"Good night, Jinx," the girls shouted together and dissolved into a fit of giggles.

A gentle rain was falling as the red pickup pulled into the parking lot. The airport was busy with people coming and going. While Mrs. Akina checked the departure board, the cousins faced each other.

"It's so hard to say good-bye," Rachel said softly.

"Well then, let's not say good-bye. Instead, let's just say aloha,'" Kanani suggested as they embraced.

"We can't say aloha," Rachel said. Her eyes filled with tears. "Aloha means 'hello'—and I'm leaving."

"That's true," Kanani agreed. "But aloha can also mean 'good-bye.' And it means 'love,' too." She paused and then said, "Aloha, Rachel."

Rachel wiped away her tears. "Aloha, Kanani."

When Kanani awoke in the morning, it took her a moment to figure out where she was. Then she remembered. She was in her own bed instead of the futon on the floor. She imagined Rachel was sleeping in her new bedroom—far away in New York.

Kanani fetched her diary and wrote,

Dear Diary,
I can't believe that Rachel is gone. Now, whenever I see a rainbow, I'm going to be reminded of the one that appeared right before her plane took off.
I miss her so much already.

After a few days, Kanani had slipped back into her old routine of eating breakfast with her mom and dad, working at Akina's for a few hours, and then hanging out with Celina for the rest of the day.

One day about a week after Rachel had left, the girls were headed toward 'Olino Cove after lunch. They each had a shave ice. With her wooden spoon, Kanani took a big scoop of bright green ice. She loved the new flavor, Rachel's Big Apple.

"I have some bad news," Celina said.

Kanani grew anxious. "What is it?"

"Seth can't take us surfing today," Celina informed her. "He's got paying customers."

Kanani shrugged. Secretly, she felt relieved. "That's okay," she replied.

"Well, it's a bummer," Celina said. "I told him how much we love surfing, and Seth promised that next time, he'll take us out extra long."

Kanani's mouth felt dry. She took another bite of shave ice.

When they reached the cove, Kanani spotted a Monk Seal Foundation volunteer sitting in a beach chair outside a large roped-off area. "Aloha, Kanani," she called out. "Look who's here!"

Kanani's heart skipped a beat when she saw Malana. Even though the seal had been showing up regularly, it was still exciting to see her every time. "Aloha, Myrtle!" Kanani said, waving. By now she knew most of the volunteers.

Seeing Malana reminded her of something. "Celina, I had a great idea—I was thinking we could print up posters telling people how to help protect the seals. We could put them up in store windows and at school."

"I'll bet my parents would put one up in the

restaurant," Celina said. "But isn't printing posters kind of expensive?"

"Yeah, you're probably right," said Kanani. "Somehow I'll have to figure that part out."

As they watched Malana sleep on the beach, the girls savored their shave ice. The soft and snowy powder melted in Kanani's mouth instantly, and the apple flavor was a tart, juicy answer to the hot summer sun. Suddenly Kanani and Celina looked at each other. "Shave ice!" they exclaimed at the same time. Quickly, they linked pinkies and pulled them apart.

"My dad has that new shave-ice cart—maybe he'll let us use it to raise money," Kanani said. "If we could set it up by the pier, we could sell shave ice at the beach. What do you think?"

"I think it's a great idea!" Celina enthused. "And that way, we'll have plenty of time for surfing, since we'll already be right at the beach."

"Surfing? Well . . . " Kanani faltered.

"I mean, now that Rachel's back in New York, you'll have more time for surfing and just hanging out at the beach, like before," said Celina.

"Well, I'm . . . I'm sure we can figure something out," Kanani stammered.

Celina's face lit up. "Kanani, I knew you felt the

same way I do about surfing. That's why we're best friends—because we're so much alike!"

Kanani didn't know what to say. Would Celina still want to be best friends if she knew that Kanani didn't really care for surfing after all?

Suddenly Kanani remembered an errand she'd been meaning to run. She stood up. "I have to get something at the minimart. You want to come with me?"

Celina was watching the surfers. "You go ahead," she said. "I'll catch up with you later."

When Kanani got home from her shopping, a postcard from Rachel was waiting for her. On the back of a photo of the Statue of Liberty, her cousin had written,

Greetings from the Big Apple! Our new apartment is wonderful. I can see Central Park from my bedroom window. There's no beach, but there's a nice lake, and I can watch horse-drawn carriages giving rides to the tourists. Yesterday we watched the sea lions getting fed at the zoo, and I thought of Malana. Have you seen her? How is she doing?
Love, Rachel

With a smile, Kanani tucked the postcard into her diary. Then she opened her shopping bag and took out a brand-new sketchbook. On the front page, she taped a photo of herself with Barksee, Mochi, and Jinx. On another page she inserted a photo of Malana. Then, on a postcard of Waipuna Beach, she wrote,

Dear Rachel,

This sketchbook is from Mochi and me to replace the one that she ate. Hey, guess what? I'm going to sell shave ice to raise money to help the monk seals. So far, Rachel's Big Apple is a bestseller!

Malana is doing great. I'm glad to hear you are too.

Aloha,

Kanani

Glossary of Hawaiian Words

aloha *(ah-LO-hah)*—hello, good-bye, love, compassion

haole *(HOW-lee)*—a white or Caucasian person

hapa *(HAH-pah)*—a part or portion, half

ho'okipa *(ho-oh-KEE-pah)*—to show hospitality

ho'opono *(ho-oh-PO-no)*—to do the right thing

humuhumunukunukuapua'a *(hoo-moo-hoo-moo-noo-koo-noo-koo-AH-poo-AH-ah)*—a reef triggerfish

kalua *(kah-LOO-ah)*—to bake in a hot pit in the ground

keiki *(KAY-kee)*—child

kukui *(koo-KOO-ee)*—a tree with large, smooth nuts

kulolo *(koo-LO-lo)*—a taro root and coconut cream custard

lau-lau *(low-low; rhymes with bow-bow)*—wrapped, such as food wrapped in leaves

lua'u *(LOO-ow)*—a Hawaiian feast

mahalo *(mah-HAH-lo)*—thank you

'ohana *(oh-HAH-nah)*—family

'ono *(OH-no)*—tasty, delicious

poi *(poy)*—a starchy pudding made from pounded taro root

puka *(POO-kah)*—hole. Puka shells have holes in the center.

shaka *(SHAH-kah)*—a hand gesture that can mean "hi," "see you later," "everything's cool," or "all right!"

taro *(TAIR-oh)*—a tropical plant with a starchy, edible root

Letter from American Girl

Dear Readers,

Just as Kanani helped save a Hawaiian monk seal that she found struggling on the beach, girls everywhere are making a big difference in the lives of animals in need. Here are the true stories of five girls around the country who did just that, each in her own special way. One looks out for sea turtles. Another helped fix a problem in the environment that was killing swans. A third nursed an injured deer back to health before setting it free. And two work tirelessly to find loving families for homeless dogs and cats.

We hope you are inspired by these real girls and their stories. As they show, there are as many ways for girls to help as there are animals who need them. The effort can be as big as starting an organization or as simple as comforting a homeless pet. Any girl can make a difference—including you!

Your friends at American Girl

Hero of the Honu

Meimei N. is a budding marine biologist from Hawai'i. The 13-year-old works with the state's green sea turtles, called *honu*, as part of a school program to help save the endangered reptiles. "I collect data at the honu pond at one of the study sites," she says. "Eight baby turtles—four boys and four girls—live in the pond."

On a typical day at the site, Meimei's first task is to pick up each turtle using a soft rubber net. She weighs it, measures its length and width, and records the numbers in her turtle data book. "Sometimes I find them basking on a sunny rock in the pond or resting under a little waterfall," she says. "I love measuring the turtles and watching them grow."

The turtles are tagged so that scientists can monitor them and understand what they need to survive. "We get to snorkel in the ocean to look for turtles," Meimei says. "They swim so fast!" When she brings a turtle back to the beach, she helps the scientists gently tag it, measure it, and check its condition before releasing it back into the water.

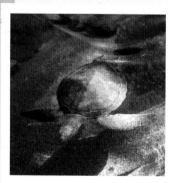

"It is exciting to be so close to the turtles," she says. "I feel really good knowing that I'm helping to save them."

Swan Support

Trumpeter swans are the largest swans in the world. One day 14-year-old Nicole H. saw one lying in the snow near her Wyoming home and realized it was not alive. It turned out that the majestic birds were dying when they flew into overhead power lines by a creek where they liked to spend the winter.

Nicole was determined to help get the power lines buried. By soliciting donations at her parents' business and giving media interviews, she raised public awareness—along with $12,000 of the $160,000 needed to bury the lines and save the swans. "I'm glad I did it," says Nicole. "It made my community a little bit stronger. I'm glad that I helped the birds, because they mean a lot to me and also to a lot of people in my hometown."

Dear to a Deer

Nichole S. and her mom brought home Bucky, a fawn that had been hit by a combine near their Ohio home and had a broken leg. Nichole's aunt works with animals and came to tend Bucky's leg, while 12-year-old Nichole and her family bottle-fed the fawn in their mudroom.

The fawn healed and grew, and eventually moved outside to the fields around Nichole's house. "Bucky came to visit us sometimes," Nichole says. "It was sad to let him go after being with him for so long, but we think he made some friends out in the field." Bucky did make friends and even started a family. One day the deer everyone thought was a boy brought *her* new twin fawns home to visit Nichole!

Dogs' Best Friend

Brook B. has a more hectic morning schedule than most girls. Before school starts, she feeds and exercises 25 dogs! The Ohio 13-year-old founded Heroes of Animals, an organization that cares for dogs without homes. She knew she had to do something when she visited a shelter that had space for only 14 pets but was trying to manage 70.

While working at pet adoption fairs, Brook met an elderly man who fostered more than two dozen dogs on his land. When he died, his house and grounds were donated to Heroes of Animals for use as a sanctuary—a place where dogs can live until they have real homes. Brook says that all her hard work is worth it when she receives letters and photos from people who have adopted her dogs—50 of them so far. "Now they're sleeping in nice beds and getting lots of attention!" she says.

Cat Crusader

"Holding a cat makes you feel warm on the inside," says 14-year-old Vanja G. After she saved an abandoned kitten from a sewer, she was inspired to help other homeless cats. Vanja took care of Panther, a lovable stray cat in her neighborhood. She volunteered at cat adoption fairs and worked at other events for a feline rescue group in her Virginia community. With Vanja's help, the rescue group saves the lives of more than 500 cats a year. "I love all animals and would do anything I could to help them if they were hurt or hungry," she says. "Just knowing a cat makes you feel good."